"Why let me go on hoping?" Talan asked

"Why don't you just admit that you can't stand the sight of me?"

Joselin's head came up. "It isn't like that at all."

"Then, for God's sake, what is it like?"

"I don't know," she said, clasping her arms around her body defensively.

His lip curled into a sneer. "You don't know. You don't know whether there's a future for us as husband and wife, and you're not even willing to give it a chance. Maybe it's just as well I didn't make love to you last night. At least now I still have a way out."

Suddenly Joselin shivered violently. Even before she'd had a chance to tell him the truth, Talan had withdrawn his mantle of love from her. She felt cold and bereft.

Valerie Parv had a busy and successful career as a journalist and advertising copywriter, before she began writing for Harlequin in 1982. She is an enthusiastic member of several Australian writers' organizations. Her many interests include her husband, her cat and the Australian environment. Her love of the land is a distinguishing feature in many of her books for Harlequin. She has recently written a colorful study in a nonfiction book titled *The Changing Face of Australia*. Her home is in New South Wales.

Books by Valerie Parv

These books may be available at your local bookseller.

Don't miss any of our special offers. Write to us at the following address for information on our newest releases.

Harlequin Reader Service
901 Fuhrmann Blvd., P.O. Box 1397, Buffalo, NY 14240
Canadian address: P.O. Box 603,
Fort Erie, Ont. L2A 9Z9

Boss
of Yarrakina
Valerie Parv

Harlequin Books

TORONTO • NEW YORK • LONDON
AMSTERDAM • PARIS • SYDNEY • HAMBURG
STOCKHOLM • ATHENS • TOKYO • MILAN

Original hardcover edition published in 1986
by Mills & Boon Limited

ISBN 0-373-02797-4

Harlequin Romance first edition November 1986

CHAPTER ONE

WITH a sigh of relief, Joselin Pride steered her low-slung sports car off the main road and on to the eucalyptus-lined driveway which led to Yarrakina homestead. Not much further now and she would be comfortably installed in the only real home she'd known since her parents divorced when she was thirteen.

On either side of the road, the setting sun spilled golden light over the titian-coloured pastures and emus grazed peacefully in the paddock to her left. The giant ostrich-like birds hardly spared her a glance as she passed.

For the first time in weeks, she felt the tight knot of tension in her stomach begin to unravel. She had been right to come here, to the one place in Australia where she could lay to rest the demons of fear which haunted her and try to regain her lost self-confidence.

Suddenly, a clay-coloured shape obscured her vision and instinctively, she hauled the steering wheel around, just missing the old man kangaroo which bounded into the centre of the road. Too late, she noticed that the road shoulder was heavily eroded. Before she could wrestle the car back on to the road, the left wheel plunged into the ditch, bringing the car to a halt at a sickening angle.

'Damn and blast!' she swore, but more out of fear than aggression. She lifted her hands from the wheel and distastefully wiped them dry on the velour seatcover. Her forehead was also filmed with moisture and as she held her hands out in front of her, they shook visibly.

5

Ineffectually, she shook a fist at the kangaroo, which still sat in the centre of the road, gazing at her with big, incurious eyes. Then it shuffled around and pronged back over the fence towards a mob of its fellows gathered under a red gum.

'That's right, just go off and leave me in this fix,' she mumbled, her voice blurring with self-pity. What an idiot she was not to have been alert to such a possibility. She hadn't spent every school holiday here since she was thirteen without learning that the kangaroos loved to rest on the sun-warmed road of an evening. They were a normal hazard of driving in the outback at sunset.

She also cursed herself for reacting so badly to what was really no more than a minor mishap. She would need help to get the car back on to the road, of course, but the homestead was only a half-hour of brisk walking away. At any other time, she would have taken the whole thing in her stride.

Except that this wasn't any other time. And her present state of mind was the very reason she had come to Yarrakina. She was fed up with over-reacting every time the slightest danger threatened.

'Like now, for instance,' she said, her voice thick with self-disgust. Here she was, in a cold sweat and trembling from head to foot, all because a kangaroo had jumped across the road in front of her.

Resignedly, she climbed out of the tilting vehicle and reached for her suitcase which lay on the back seat. Thanking her lucky stars that she had worn low-heeled boots, she set off down the road towards the homestead.

The sun had almost disappeared behind the spectacular sandstone ridges of the Grampians by the time she reached the house. Surprisingly, it was still deserted. She had expected her aunt to be home for

dinner, and the men to be coming in from the fields by
now. Not that their absence worried her unduly.
Spring was a busy time on a sheep station, and her
aunt was fond of exploring the aboriginal cave
paintings which honeycombed the Grampians, so she
was often away for long periods. Since she knew the
region like the back of her hand, Joselin never
worried, even though her aunt was in her seventies.

Joselin's boot heels clip-clopped on the tallow-wood
verandah and she smiled at the familiar cree-eak of the
insect-screen door as she pushed it open. But as she
snapped on the living room light, she froze, her eyes
wide.

The creaking door was about the only thing she
recognised. Without so much as giving her a hint in
her letters, her aunt had redecorated the entire
homestead.

The convict-made bricks lining the walls were the
same but the pine floorboards had been covered by
thick oatmeal carpeting and the comfortable old chintz
suite Joselin remembered had been replaced by a pair
of modern sofas covered in slub linen with a vast
onyx-topped coffee table in between. The Carrara
marble fireplaces were still there—created by Italian
craftsmen in the eighteen-eighties, they were part of
the homestead's history—but the hand-moulded
ceilings and cornices had been picked out in a
stunning plum colour which, though unexpected, was
totally in keeping with the room's new look.

Once she got over her initial surprise, Joselin had to
admit that her aunt had done an amazing job, although
she had shown no special decorating skills until now.
Maybe she had called in a professional. Whatever the
explanation, it was a splendid result. Nevertheless,
Joselin felt hurt that she had been excluded from her
aunt's plans. She was also unsettled by the changes

when comforting familiarity had been one reason for
coming here.

Since there was nothing she could do about it now,
she hefted her suitcase in one hand and climbed the
wide timber staircase to her room. It was always kept
in readiness for her visits, infrequent though they had
become since she left school—she thought with a
twinge of guilt.

Pushing open her bedroom door, she gasped in
amazement. Even here, her aunt had wrought a total
transformation. Gone was the high old-fashioned
bedstead, replaced by a queen-sized ensemble topped
by a continental quilt. The curtains and quilt were
in peach colour, contrasting with the walls which
were painted in forest green. Only the adjoining
bathroom was at all familiar, its cream enamel
fixtures still in place, but highlighted by glossy
green tiles and paint on walls and ceilings. A
shaggy cream bathroom carpet covered the old-fashioned floor tiles and invited Joselin to wriggle her
bare toes in its luxuriant pile.

Dismayed, she returned to the bedroom and sank on
to the quilt. It was too much! How could her aunt
change everything she had held dear, without even
letting her know! Maybe that was why Aunt Pixie
hadn't answered the letter she sent to say she was
coming. Aunt Pixie hated scenes of any kind.

In a mutinous frame of mind. she unpacked only her
toilet things and a change of clothes, not sure whether
she would be staying after this. The kangaroo must
have been an omen because the visit was turning out
far differently from what she expected.

She felt a little better after a warm shower. The
sight of herself clad in slim-legged cord jeans and
double-breasted western shirt was reassuring.
Unpinning her hair, she let the golden curls cascade to

her shoulders and began to brush them methodically, losing herself in the familiar ritual.

Outside, there came the sound of car motors revving and dogs barking. The men must be returning from the fields. She knew the sounds almost by heart. First they would disperse to the showers to sluice away the day's grime, then they would congregate in their dining room for several rounds of icy foaming beer and a hearty evening meal.

The front door slammed and she sat up, smiling. Aunt Pixie must have returned with the men. Eagerly, she tossed the brush aside and started down the staircase to greet her favourite relative.

She froze, her heart pounding, as she caught sight of a tall, solidly built man turning from the foyer into the living room. He was a total stranger. At once, the alien and hated sense of panic returned and she crept down the staircase, shrinking back against the railing in fear that he would come out again and discover her.

He might well be an employee of her aunt's but if so, what was he doing in the house? The men all knew their presence here was by invitation only, and no one resented a rule which was designed to protect an elderly widow living alone.

Her bare feet made no sound on the slate floor as she flitted across the hall and pressed herself against the door jamb, peering cautiously through the crack between door and frame.

From here, she glimpsed an immensely broad back across which a checked shirt stretched taut, hinting at a muscular physique underneath. He was helping himself to Aunt Pixie's scotch.

Then, glass in hand, he walked back across the room, obviously intending to come into the hall. Acting on pure instinct fuelled by fear, Joselin reached for a knobbed walking stick which had been kept in the hallway for as long as she could remember.

As the man ducked slightly to step into the hall, she brought the heavy stick crashing down across his shoulders. There was the sound of shattering glass as his drink hit the slate tiles, then he joined it there, his massive frame slumped and lifeless.

Shaking, Joselin stepped over him and half-ran across the living room to the telephone. Her fingers refused to co-operate as she tried to dial the operator's number to ask for help. Only then, she realised it would be quicker to run next door to the men's dining room, but as she whirled to translate the thought into action, a grip like iron clamped over her wrist, forcing her to replace the phone.

Her eyes flared wide as she looked up into the man's piercing blue-black eyes under bushy eyebrows. With a strength she hadn't known she possessed, she wrenched herself free and backed across the room, simultaneously picking up a brass lamp from a table. 'Don't you dare touch me or I'll scream the place down,' she vowed, her trembling voice belying her brave words.

He stayed where he was, massaging the back of his neck with one hand. 'After that performance, I'd say that I should be the one calling for help, wouldn't you?'

If he was trying to catch her off guard he was succeeding. Defiantly, she repeated, 'I told you, I'll scream if you make a move. What are you—some kind of burglar, rapist or what?'

He took a half-step forward but stopped when she hefted the lamp higher, and spread his hands wide in a placatory gesture. 'In the first place, I've never had to resort to rape. My women are usually willing enough. And in the second place, why would I need to burgle my own home?'

She ignored the first comment although, looking at him, she didn't doubt that he could have his pick of women. It was his second comment which startled her. '*Your* home? You'll have to do better than that,' she snorted, but with an edge of uncertainty in her voice.

'I see. What story would you prefer then?'

Now she was getting somewhere. 'You can start by telling me what you've done with my aunt.'

A flicker of understanding lit his dark eyes. 'Your aunt? You mean Pixie Pride?'

'You've laid seige to her house and you aren't even sure of her name?'

He chuckled throatily. 'My my, we are melo-dramatic, aren't we—Joselin Pride.'

A thrill of fear coursed through her, mixed with something else disturbing and undefinable at the soft, caressing way he said her name. 'How do you know who I am?' she asked.

'Because as I said, this is my house. I bought Yarrakina from your aunt three months ago.'

Uncertainty made her lower the lamp a little. 'You bought it? How come she didn't say anything to me about selling out?'

'I'd say because you weren't sufficiently interested to find out,' he said derisively, the caressing tone completely gone. 'How long is it since you came to visit your aunt?'

She felt her cheeks flood with shameful colour. 'More than three months. But I've been . . .'

He didn't let her finish. 'Busy. I know. Like most kids your age, you think your own life is so much more important than anybody else's, especially an old lady like Pixie.'

She had been about to say she had been in hospital, and convalescing after that—none of which she had told Aunt Pixie for fear of worrying her unduly when there was nothing she could have done to help anyway. But she was damned if she was going to explain herself to this arrogant stranger who thought he could just take over a property which had been in the same family for six generations. All the changes must be his handiwork. And he had the nerve to accuse her of being insensitive! 'You seem to know a lot about me,' she said as coolly as she could through her mounting fury.

'I know you're in the film business—Pixie told me that much,' he admitted. 'I suppose you're an actress. You certainly look like one, all dolled up like that.'

She wasn't an actress but she wasn't giving him the satisfaction of admitting what her job was in the film industry, or had been until the last few months. He was right about her clothes, though. They were all from a leading Melbourne designer and although they were supposed to be country wear, the shiny leather and wool plaids that made up the collection had never been nearer to the outback than the première of *The Man From Snowy River*.

With exaggerated care, she set the lamp down on the table. 'Very well, You've criticised my career, my clothes and my attitude. Don't you think you owe me at least an introduction so I know who my critic is?'

'Touché,' he said softly. 'I'm Talan Devereaux. We've met, years ago and you know some of my family. They used to own a property in the valley before the sixties' bushfires burnt them out.'

Her eyes went round. 'Aunt Pixie's godson,' she breathed. 'I can't believe it.' The last time she had seen him was at a family Christmas gathering when she had been thirteen and he a lanky eighteen-year-old proudly sporting a wispy embryo moustache. Their families had lost touch when he and his mother had moved away from the valley—his father was buried on the property, a victim of the bushfires.

'I have changed a little I hope,' he said ruefully, massaging his jaw with one hand. 'You certainly have.'

She would hope so! If she remembered that Christmas correctly, she had been in pigtails tied with grossgrain ribbons, and had been wearing a horrid 'best' dress of cream lace. She had been fat, too, and ... now she had it ... Talan had teased her unmercifully for finishing the last of the cream cakes.

'You haven't lost your mean streak,' she growled, remembering how humiliated she had been when he caught her eating the cakes as fast as she could from behind the shelter of the table. To this day, she felt a surge of guilt every time she touched a cream cake.

'Well, you were being a greedy little pig,' he chuckled, evidently remembering the incident as clearly as she did. 'I see you haven't lost your talent for defending yourself, though.' He flexed his shoulders meaningfully and winced.

At once, she felt a rush of contrition. She had attacked him at the Christmas party, too, butting him with her bent head, until his best shirt and trousers were smeared with cream from her face and hands. But this time, she must really have hurt him. 'I'm sorry about hitting you over the head,' she said sincerely. 'Can I do anything ... get you anything?'

'Another scotch,' he said shortly. 'The last one is all over the hall floor.'

'I said I'm sorry.' She went to where she had seen him mix his drink. While he watched, she poured scotch into the glass and added ice cubes from a small built-in refrigerator, then handed him the drink.

'Won't you have one?' he asked, accepting it.

'No thanks. I should be going.'

'Going where?'

'I'll have to try and get a room in town. Now that Yarrakina no longer belongs to my aunt, I have no right to intrude on your home. I . . . I'm afraid I've already made myself far more at home here than I should have.'

He set his drink down and regarded her levelly. 'What are you planning to use for transport?'

Her car! She had forgotten about running it into the ditch. He must have seen it on the way back to the homestead. 'I swerved to dodge a kangaroo,' she explained. 'I'll need some help to get my car back in the road, then I can be on my way.'

He nodded. 'No problem. I'll send someone out to move it for you in the morning.'

'In the morning? But . . .'

'Look,' he said with exaggerated patience, 'my men have been out all day lamb marking. I can't drag them out again now just to please you.'

'Then you'll have to lend me a vehicle,' she said flatly. Surely he could see why she couldn't stay here? There were other people on the property, but she baulked at the idea of spending even one night under his roof where they were basically alone.

At her peremptory tone, his eyes narrowed and fire blazed in their dark depths. 'I don't *have* to do anything,' he said steadily, his tone vibrant with unspoken warning.

At once she regretted putting her request so badly. 'All right, I'm sorry if it sounded like an order,' she breathed, 'but I really do need your help. I don't even know my aunt's new address or how I'm going to get to her or . . . or anything.'

Mortified, she turned her head away before he could see the tears which welled up in her eyes. Self-pity was a novel emotion to her but one which she had experienced far too often lately. She jerked back as a square of lemon-scented cloth was thrust under her nose.

'Here, take this,' Talan said roughly. 'Have a good blow and pull yourself together.'

She accepted his handkerchief and did as instructed. Oddly enough, she did feel more in control of herself a moment later. 'I'm sorry,' she repeated. 'I'm not usually such a crybaby.'

'I'm glad to hear it. Frankly, I haven't much time for weepy women. My mother made a speciality of it to get what she wanted. I watched her practice on my father while I was growing up and he never seemed to realise how he was being manipulated.'

'Perhaps he loved her too much to care,' she said softly, intrigued in spite of her concern for her own predicament.

'Typical female comment,' he snorted. 'You think that love excuses everything including lying and conniving.'

What a cynic he was! Fleetingly, she wondered whether some woman had brought him to this state. His mother had apparently started it by being so manipulative, but she wondered if there was something else in his experience which had made him so distrustful of women and their ways. She shrugged away her interest. His prejudices were no concern of hers. All she cared about right now was how she was going to get away from Yarrakina tonight.

Her hopes were soon dashed. 'Even if I lent you the utility, you'd never be able to find your way back to the main road in the dark,' he observed.

He was right, she admitted despondently. Even seasoned stockmen had been known to get lost on the network of wheel tracks which criss-crossed the huge property. One wrong turning and she was likely to find herself in a creek. 'It seems as though I don't have any choice but to stay,' she said resignedly.

'Sensible girl.' He drained his whisky glass and stood up. 'Like that drink now?'

'I'll have mineral water if you have it,' she conceded. Her throat felt scratchy and dry after the tiring drive.

'Afraid you'll end up dancing on the table?' he asked, amusement lighting his eyes.

'I don't drink very much,' she said dismissively. She had been partial to a drink or two but that was before. Now, it was all she could do to function normally when she was stone cold sober. He handed her a tall glass of clear sparkling liquid in which spun a twist of fresh lemon and she sipped it gratefully. 'Thanks. This is good.'

When he remained standing, she looked up at him questioningly. 'Aren't you having one with me?'

'One before dinner's my limit,' he explained. 'Besides, in case you haven't noticed, I'm not exactly dressed for socialising. I was on my way to change when you . . . introduced yourself.' He fingered the back of his head significantly.

Only now, she noticed that he was dressed in workmanlike dark drill trousers and a faded western shirt of brushed cotton, both of which carried a distinct odour of damp wool. Dried mud caked the lower half of his trousers and his work boots were heavily scuffed. He looked as if he had put in a hard day.

Nevertheless, he was still the most attractive looking man she'd seen in a long while—the movie stars she knew included. Most of the actors, she worked with were good looking, some very much so, but it was usually superficial and palled when one realised their main preoccupation was with themselves. Such self-conscious good looks had never appealed to Joselin. But Talan's looks were *real*. His muscles were moulded through hard physical labour, not from working out in a gym, and his mahogany tan which gave his skin such a smooth patina came from the sun, not from a ray lamp.

'Do I pass muster?' he asked.

'I wasn't staring at you,' she lied, confused by his bluntness. 'I was ... thinking about my aunt.'

'Liar,' he chuckled. 'But full marks for trying. Go ahead and look if you want to. I certainly intend to.'

Her skin burned as he began a leisurely appraisal of her trim figure. In his eyes, she could see appreciation for her long, slender body, high rounded breasts and compact curves, honed from years of physical activity. Unconsciously, she half-turned her head, exposing a beautiful profile which was saved from classic regularity by wide-set eyes which had been described to her as having the brilliance of an underlit pool.

Many times, she had been appraised by a director, seeking to assess her suitability for a job. But this inspection was infinitely more personal—and disturbing. She felt as if he was reaching a decision about her, and wondered what it was.

In self-defence, she began to study him feature by feature, noting the lithe, lean body he carried with such self-assurance, the wide expanse of shoulders and proud carriage of his head on a substantial neck. Her courage almost failed her when she reached his face, but she willed herself to meet his wry gaze. His mouth was firm and well shaped and there was a trace of shadow on the jutting jaw. His nose was high bridged and uneven, as if it had once been broken but the effect was distinguished rather than ugly.

In fact, there was nothing about him she could call ugly, she realised, arriving at last at those disturbing eyes under their bushy brows. Coloured an unusual blue-black, they seemed to probe into her very soul. Shaken, she looked away.

'If either of us goes missing, we should be able to give the police an excellent description,' he murmured, his tone faintly mocking.

'You're impossible!' she seethed. 'I don't even know what I'm doing here.'

'Looking me up and down to see if tonight is going to prove interesting,' he ventured. 'Isn't that what film people usually do?'

Instantly she bristled. 'You don't know the first thing about film people—or me, for that matter. I'm not given to ... to one-night stands, if that's what you're implying.'

'I'm not implying it. I'm stating the fact,' he went on. 'I dated an actress once and she told me how uninhibited you all are.'

So that's where he had polished his veneer of cynicism! 'Weren't you going to get changed or something?' she asked icily. 'Besides, if you believed so readily in type-casting, you would have to be a hayseed-chomping oaf! Oh! I'm sorry, I shouldn't have said that,' she added, horrified by her own rudeness, even though it was provoked.

'I admit I deserved that,' he conceded, his eyes dancing with laughter. 'All right, I'm going, but I will be back.'

'Can I start preparing dinner or something?' she asked, feeling useless—and also feeling a strong urge to prove to him that she was more mature and capable than he believed.

'The head stockman's wife, Lillian, comes in to cook for me,' he explained. 'Her eldest daughter, Jean, helps with the housework and the dishes, so there's no cause for you to worry.'

'You've got your harem all organised, haven't you?'

she muttered under her breath but dared not repeat it aloud. Instead, she said, 'At least give me Aunt Pixie's new phone number so I can call her and let her know where I am.'

'She's not expecting you, if that's on your mind,' he said. Seeing her baffled expression, he relented somewhat. 'I wasn't going to tell you until you'd had something to eat and a rest, but your aunt hasn't moved into town. She's in hospital.'

Her hand flew to her face in dismay. 'She's ill? Why didn't you say something sooner? You let me think everything was all right . . .'

'Easy girl,' he said in a tone he might use to soothe a nervous horse. 'She *is* all right, and she's in the best place for her right now. Look, it's a long story and I'd really like to get out of these work clothes. Will you try to restrain your curiosity—and your panic—until I can fill you in properly?'

Annoyed at the suggestion that she was panicking, she nodded dully. 'As long as I have your word that she's in no danger for the moment.'

He rested a hand on her shoulder and the warmth of his skin seared her through her shirt. 'You have my word.'

All the same, she paced restlessly up and down the living room while she waited for him to come back. Only a serious illness would have persuaded Aunt Pixie to part with Yarrakina, even to her godson.

Miserably, she wrung her hands together. If only she'd made the effort to come back sooner, she would have found out what was wrong in time to . . . to do what? In her present state of mind, it was all she could do to make decisions affecting her own life, far less help Pixie with her problems. She only wished she could explain her reasons for neglecting Pixie to Talan. He obviously thought she was self-centred and unfeeling.

Yet any sort of explanation would involve telling him what had happened to her over the last few months and she didn't feel up to that yet. 'Get away somewhere where you won't have to explain what you do for a living,' her doctor had advised her. 'That way, you can give in to your need to be protected without everyone expecting you to be daring and strong.'

If only things had worked out that way. She couldn't expect any pampering from Talan. He had made it clear that he disliked weak women. And her aunt was in no position to look after her, when Pixie needed care herself. So what was she going to do now?

She looked up as Talan came back into the room. His hair stood up in shower-damp spikes and he had changed into straight-legged chambray jeans and a cream knitted shirt which hugged his torso and outlined every muscle in stark relief. As he entered the room, she caught a whiff of musky after-shave which surprised her. She hadn't expected a sheep farmer to be so sophisticated.

He shrugged expressively. 'See. The hayseeds do wash off.'

A warm glow crept over her cheeks and she ducked her head. 'For goodness' sake, stop reading my mind.'

He grinned. 'If I could do that, I would have saved myself a lot of pain.'

Her head came up. 'I hope I didn't do any damage. I really thought you were an intruder here.'

'It's all right. I'll have a bruise across my shoulders but it isn't the first time. You didn't know what changes had taken place since you were last here.'

'I was going to explain about that,' she began tentatively but he forestalled her.

'You don't owe me any explanations. You're entitled to live your own life.' He didn't sound as if he believed that at all but she didn't want to quarrel with him. She was more anxious to know what had happened to Pixie.

'I'll tell you the whole story over dinner,' he said, frustrating her. 'Lillian has left us a casserole in the oven. She asked if we minded doing our own cleaning up tonight since Jean is away for a few days.'

So they were alone in the big house. For some reason, Joselin found this discovery disquieting but she kept her worries to herself, not wanting to give him any ideas. 'I'll be glad to help clean up,' she assured him as she followed him into the dining room.

She waited impatiently as he ladled steak and kidney on to their plates and offered her a basket of steaming bread which was fragrant with garlic butter. After accepting some she set it down. 'For goodness' sake, will you tell me what's happened to Pixie?'

His expression didn't change. 'I don't know about you, but I'm ravenous. When I wasn't out mustering today, I was lending a hand with the lamb marking. That sort of work gives one an appetite.'

She could take a hint. Smouldering with impatience, she tried to follow his example and eat her food but she could only pick at it, while he cleared everything on his plate. After an age, he mopped up the last of the gravy with his bread and downed it appreciatively, then pushed the plate away. 'Now, we can talk without ruining our appetites.'

Hers was already ruined by his silence but she kept quiet, not wanting to divert him any longer. 'Pixie has a bad heart,' he said at last. 'Her doctor recommends surgery.'

Her eyes widened. 'But that's very serious, isn't it?'

He nodded. 'Without the operation, she would die.'

'But you said she was in no danger.'

'I said for the moment, which is true,' he reminded her.

'Why didn't she tell me anything was wrong? I always thought she was in perfect health.'

'So she was, until the last year or so. Unbeknown to any of us, she's been on medication for months and her condition has been steadily deteriorating. I only noticed there was anything wrong when I came to live here, three months ago.'

'Is that why you stayed?'

'It's the main reason. I came back with the idea of buying a place in the valley, never dreaming it would be Yarrakina. When I found out how ill Pixie was, I suggested buying her out and she agreed, so I was able to stay on here and take care of her. Of course, I didn't put it like that to her. You know how she is? I had to let her think she was the one taking care of the poor helpless bachelor.'

Anyone less helpless than Talan, Joselin couldn't imagine but she could see how Aunt Pixie would fall for the line. She had been raised believing that women existed for the sole purpose of caring for their menfolk. No man ever washed a dish or made a bed while she had the strength to do it for them. 'Women's work is women's work,' she would affirm when Joselin protested that the men were capable of looking after themselves.

'I'm glad you were here,' she said softly, feeling guiltier than ever for staying away so long. 'It's a miracle you could persuade her to leave you long enough to have the operation.'

Talan drew a pattern with his knife on the tablecloth. 'I wasn't able to persuade her. She only agreed to go to hospital because I intercepted your letter and told her you were coming to look after me.'

Which explained why Aunt Pixie hadn't replied to her letter. 'I see,' Joselin said slowly. 'It must have been a blow to her principles to have to allow us to stay here together, unchaperoned.'

'It would have been. In fact, I think she would still have refused to go to hospital but for one thing.'

A premonition of disaster set Joselin's heart thudding in her chest. 'And what was that?'

'I told her you and I were engaged to be married.'

CHAPTER TWO

SHE stared at him, open-mouthed. 'You told her *what*?'

'You heard me. Look, Joselin, she must have that operation and she wouldn't go until she knew I was taken care of. You know she'd never let us share the house unless we were about to be married, so I was left with no choice.'

Even though she was still stunned by his confession, she could see his point. Aunt Pixie wouldn't dream of leaving him alone with no woman to look after him, yet neither would she agree to let two unattached people share the same house. Joselin's letter must have been the answer to Talan's prayers. Thank goodness she hadn't revealed the reason why she wanted to come back, preferring to tell Aunt Pixie face to face. 'I see why you had to tell her we were engaged,' she conceded.

Relief lightened his dark eyes. 'Then you'll play your part?'

Could she pretend to be Talan's loving fiancée long enough to convince her aunt to have the operation? 'Of course I will,' she said at once. 'What will I have to do?'

'Just come to the hospital with me and go along with whatever I say about our relationship. Once we've set her mind at rest, she will have the operation. Then, afterwards, we can make a show of changing our minds. It won't be the first time an engagement was called off.'

A pang shot through Joselin at his easy come, easy

go attitude. Whatever the circumstances, it didn't seem right to be planning the end of an engagement before it had even begun. 'There's one other small matter,' she volunteered.

'What's that?'

She held up her left hand which was innocent of any rings. 'We'd better do something about this, Pixie's bound to notice if I'm not wearing a ring.'

His mouth twisted into a cynical smile. 'So that's the price of your co-operation, is it?'

Instantly, she bridled. 'It's no such thing. I just meant I'll need a ring for show. You'll get it back as soon as this is over. Whatever you may think of me, I'd do anything for Pixie. After my parents split up this was the only home I had. In many ways, she was more like a mother to me than my own mother.'

At once, his hard expression relaxed and something very like compassion softened his angular features. 'I'm sorry, I shouldn't have said what I did. I feel the same way about Pixie for my own reasons. After Dad was killed in the bushfire, Mum sold out and took us to Canberra where she has relatives, but she was never the same after that. With no one to prop her up, she just sort of . . . faded away. The doctors put her death down to something else of course, but without Dad, she was like a house whose foundations had eroded away.'

'And Pixie backed you up through it all?'

'As steady as Ayers Rock. She told me I was wasted in the city, teaching, even if it was at an Agricultural College. She said I'd never be happy until I was back on the land—and she was right. Here I am.'

Instinctively, Joselin stretched out a hand to him, then drew it back self-consciously. Maybe he wouldn't welcome her sympathy. 'It hasn't turned out the way you planned though, has it?' she asked instead.

His wandering gaze shifted back to focus on her with disturbing intensity. 'No, it hasn't—although I can't say I'm unhappy as the boss of Yarrakina. It's the finest property in the Wimmera. But I wish it had come about through happier circumstances.' The tight beam of his gaze grew even more penetrating. 'I get the feeling that your visit isn't turning out the way you planned, either. Why did you come back? Your letter didn't give any clues.'

Her skin felt hot as she looked away, not sure enough of him yet to reveal the deeply personal reasons why she was here. 'I just felt I needed a rest,' she dissembled.

'I should have thought a Barrier Reef island would be more to an actress's taste than an isolated sheep station.'

'There you go again, jumping to conclusions. I practically grew up here so why shouldn't I look on Yarrakina as home ... I mean, I did while it belonged to Pixie.'

'You can still treat it as home, you know. Especially since you're about to be its mistress.'

Pain flickered in her eyes and she blinked away the mistiness. 'Temporary, acting mistress-elect, don't forget.'

His sigh was unexpected. 'Of course. Purely temporary.' He pushed his chair back from the table and stood up. 'Stay here, I'll be back in a second.'

Curiously, she watched him go, noting again the instinctive ducking of his head as he went through the doorway. The doorways at Yarrakina were high enough for him to walk through unbowed, but the gesture was too ingrained, and marked him as a man accustomed to standing taller than his surroundings.

A few minutes later, he returned carrying a small velvet-covered box which he opened and offered to her. Inside was an exquisite heart-shaped ruby set on an antique gold band. 'It's lovely,' she breathed.

'I doubt whether it will fit, but let's try it.' He took her left hand in his, splaying the fingers so he could slip the ring on to her third finger. 'Amazing,' he muttered. 'My grandmother had the smallest hands I've ever seen, and yet the ring fits you perfectly.'

So the ring was a family heirloom, she thought as she admired it winking brightly on her finger. Her hands weren't really small, but they were fine-boned. All at once, she became conscious of his hand still cupping hers and she drew back. 'Thank you. It will do the job nicely.'

His eyebrow winged upwards at an ironic angle. 'How romantic.'

'Well, what did you expect? We're only doing this for Pixie's sake, after all.'

'Of course. We mustn't forget that, must we?'

Why did she get the feeling he would like to? But he couldn't possibly feel anything for her. They barely knew each other. Their visits to the property had often coincided but she had seen very little of him. He was so much older that their friends and their interests were completely different. After that fateful family Christmas party their paths hadn't crossed again, although Aunt Pixie had mentioned him in her letters occasionally.

Which brought her to another problem. 'Pixie's been writing to both of us. Won't she think this is suspiciously sudden?'

'I anticipated that and told her we've been meeting secretly in Melbourne to avoid getting her hopes up until we were sure of our feelings for each other. Which is why I want you to back me up when we talk to her.'

How well he knew Pixie! 'She must be thrilled

about her two strays getting together,' she said wryly, 'but it will be a blow to her when we split up.'

'At least by then she'll be out of danger. You aren't getting cold feet about this, are you?'

'No, of course not. It's just . . .'

'Just what?'

How could she explain the wistful feeling which crept over her at the sight of the ring sparkling on her finger? After the mess her parents made of their marriage, she hoped things would turn out differently for her. Her dreams certainly didn't include this—this travesty of an engagement. However worthy their motives might be, she couldn't make herself feel good about it. 'Nothing,' she said, since he was waiting for her to finish.

'In that case, we'd better clear this lot away.'

So much for romance, she thought sourly as she helped him to clear the table and load the dishes into the automatic dishwasher which was another new addition since her last visit. Feeling an urgent need to be alone, she declined Talan's invitation to listen to some records with him, and went to her own room.

She was too keyed up to go straight to bed, so she changed into a sheer pink chiffon nightie and matching *peignoir*. Her clothes—chosen mostly for work—were usually unfussy and practical, almost masculine, she had been told, but she compensated by buying the sheerest most luxurious underwear and nightwear. If her fellow stunt people ever saw the off-duty Joselin Pride, no doubt they would laugh themselves silly.

In the act of tying the satin ribbon at her throat, she froze. My God, this was the first time she had thought about her work since she got here' She had been so caught up in Pixie's problems and Talan's drastic solution that she hadn't given her own worries a thought.

Pensively, she bit her lip. Her distraction was only temporary. As soon as she switched off the light, back would come the feeling of dread, which she'd lived with since the accident.

Although it was three months ago now, she remembered every detail of the night it had happened. She and stunt co-ordinator Terry Haines had been working late setting up a stunt scene for the next day's filming, returning to the motel hours after the rest of the crew. Terry was a superb driver, one of the best in the business, but even his defensive skills were useless against a drunk behind the wheel of a powerful sports car. The man was weaving all over the road and, dodging him, Terry's car had gone over a sheer drop. A tree branch came through the front windscreen, breaking their fall but battering Terry cruelly. He died instantly, leaving Joselin pinned in the car, wondering with every creak of the tree when it would give way and hurtle her to the valley below.

It was hours before a passing motorist spotted their car and summoned help. By then, Joselin was hysterical with pain and fear, and the horror of being trapped alongside Terry's mutilated body.

She had recovered, at least physically, miraculously having sustained no more than bruises and a small fracture. She had been hurt far worse on the job and bounced back. It was her spirit which refused to heal.

The first she knew of this was when she accepted a straightforward stunt job—jumping from a fifth-floor window on to a prepared pile of empty cardboard cartons. She'd done similar high falls hundreds of times. Except that this time, her feet refused to launch her off the ledge. After two such fiascos, word spread that Joselin Pride had lost her nerve. No more job offers were forthcoming.

'Get away where nobody expects anything of you.

Give your mind a chance to heal,' her doctor finally
advised her.

Yet here she was, expected to act as fiancée to a
man she barely knew, with little alternative if she
was to save the life of the person she loved most in
the world.

A strangled sob brought her out of her reverie and
she was startled to see her face in the mirror, reflecting
the pain and torment which gave rise to the sob. How
could she possibly give such a demanding performance
when she barely possessed the inner resources to keep
going?

'Think of Pixie,' she told her reflection, and was
gratified to see her eyes lose some of their haunted
expression. Maybe if she kept Pixie firmly in mind,
her love for the elderly woman would sustain her
through the ordeal.

What she would do if anything happened to Pixie,
she hated to think. She was the closest person to
Joselin in the world. After her parents' divorce,
Joselin's father had gone jackarooing in the Outback
and his letters were intermittent, the last coming from
a property in North Queensland. Her mother had
married again, to a man closer to Joselin's age than her
own and who plainly resented Joselin's presence. So
she had no one.

The light caught the gem on her finger and it
flashed fire into her eyes. Except that now she had a
fiancée, she reminded herself. The thought of Talan
Devereaux, so strong and confident, made her smile. If
only they were truly in love and the ring was for real!

She made a face at her reflection. If her doctor was
right and she did have a deep-seated yearning to be
protected, it wouldn't do her any good to fix her sights
on Talan. He had made it clear that he had no time for
weak women, and his interest in her was purely

practical. She had problems enough without turning down that particular dead-end.

Determined to escape from her worrisome thoughts, she buried her head in a new thriller she'd bought before leaving Melbourne, and read until it was late enough to risk getting into bed. Nervously, she reached for the light switch and snapped it off, tensing as darkness closed in on her. But it was soon replaced by silver threads of moonlight, trailing across the room and, reassured, she relaxed enough to sleep.

It seemed only minutes before she was opening her eyes again and blinking at the brilliant sunshine streaming into her room. She was still getting her bearings when the door opened and Talan strode in, cup in hand. 'I thought you might like this, since today is rather special—our betrothal day, so to speak.'

Her fervent hope that she'd dreamed yesterday's events was in vain then. She really had agreed to pose as his fiancée. 'What time shall we go to the hospital?' she asked a little faintly.

'Straight after breakfast. Pixie's doctor told me she mustn't put off the operation for much longer or it may be too late.'

As she reached for the cup, the blanket fell away, exposing the chiffon nightie which barely covered her silken flesh. Since she couldn't retrieve the blanket without spilling the tea, she pretended not to mind how much he could see of her and she was uncomfortably aware that he made the most of the opportunity. 'Do you mind?' she asked stiffly when she could at last set the cup down and cover herself decently again.

He was unperturbed. 'Not at all. I was just admiring my choice of a fiancée in fact. I have excellent taste, wouldn't you say?'

'Since you had very little choice, I wouldn't know,'

she responded acidly then realised how rude she sounded when all he did was to pay her a compliment. She wasn't usually so touchy. 'I'm sorry, I'm not at my best first thing.'

He shrugged. 'Who is? But you'd better be at your best when we reach the hospital. I won't stand for any tricks where Pixie's well-being is concerned.'

Since he already knew how much Pixie meant to her, he wasn't being very fair. 'I'll play my part as agreed,' she told him.

When he left, she drank the tea quickly then threw back the covers and bounded out of bed. Despite Talan's surliness which she generously put down to worry over Pixie, she felt younger and more carefree than she'd done in months. Yarrakina was already working its magic on her, it seemed.

Soon afterwards, she joined Talan downstairs to find him frying bacon and eggs for two. He gave an approving nod to her choice of red tartan trousers and cream hand-knitted jacket over a red T-shirt, and set a plate of food down in front of her. 'Don't expect service like this every day. Usually, I'm away to the paddocks at dawn.'

Instantly, she tensed. 'I didn't expect it today, and I'm perfectly capable of getting my own breakfast.' She knew what he was thinking—that her looks and clothes pointed to a scatterbrained actress who was incapable of doing anything domestic. By his own admission, that made her beneath his contempt.

She was tempted to tell him there and then what she really did for a living—let him think she was a clinging vine *then*! In time, she remembered her doctor's injunction and bit her lip pretending great interest in the food on her plate.

'I hope it's to your liking,' he said, noticing her hesitation.

'It's fine thanks. More than I usually eat for breakfast.'

His disgust was immediately apparent. 'Mustn't spoil that perfect figure, must we?'

'I'm not a narcissic type who worries over every ounce,' she defended herself. 'Usually I eat like a horse.'

'A thoroughbred filly, I'll be bound,' he retorted.

At once, she put her knife and fork down and rested her chin on one hand, so their eyes collided. 'Why are you being such a beast this morning?'

'I wasn't aware that I was.'

'Well you are. I've agreed to fall in with your plans to help my aunt, so it shouldn't matter whether you approve of me or not.'

His eyes clouded slightly. 'Then why does it?'

She was asking herself the same question and could come up with no convincing answer. 'It . . . it doesn't really. But I could play the part of your fiancée better if you didn't keep picking on me all the time.'

His smile curved outwards from the centre of his mouth to the corners, giving the impression that the sun had come out in the room. 'I see, a method actress. You feel it's important to really live your role.'

This wasn't what she had meant at all, she thought with alarm as he rose and walked around to her side of the table. 'What . . . what are you doing?' she asked as he took both her hands and urged her to her feet.

'Just helping you to get into character—*darling*.' There was no need to ask what he meant because his tightening embrace made it all too clear. His mouth, when it closed over hers, was warm and firm, demanding a response that she was powerless to withhold. Nor did she want to, for the fiery sensation which tore through her at his touch was much too new and exciting. Her job seldom called for love scenes—

stunts and romance being mutually exclusive—so she
felt herself lacking in practice, but from somewhere deep
inside her came the responses she found herself making.

Her hands wandered over his broad back, revelling
in the sculptured feel of his body and she pressed close
against him as the pressure of his lips aroused in her a
desperate sense of hunger that she knew instinctively
no food in the world could satisfy.

Her eyes, closed until now, fluttered open and her
long lashes grazed his cheeks. Then she hastily closed
them against the burning expression in his eyes. What
was he thinking about, to look so fierce and primitive?
She was sure he wasn't sharing her amazed sense of
arousal. No man had ever made her feel this way
before.

So she was all the more shattered when he pushed
her back into her chair. Her breathing was laboured
and her breasts heaved visibly through the T-shirt,
but he seemed completely in control of himself—if it
wasn't for that smouldering expression in his eyes
which, even as she watched, faded and died. 'Talan
. . .' she began breathlessly, searching to put into
words the torrent of feelings his embrace had aroused.

He dismissed her emotional turmoil with a sharp
gesture. 'I can see you really do like to get into a
character. Maybe now, you'll be able to play your part
successfully at the hospital.'

Disappointment tore through her like a knife thrust.
'Is that the only reason you kissed me?'

'What other reason could there be?'

'I thought maybe you felt something for me.'

His explosive laugh was even more cruel than his
casual response to her kiss. 'Good heavens, woman! I
told you I've no time for clinging females—actresses
especially.'

Defiantly, she thrust her chin forward. 'What if I

wasn't an actress?'

'Since we both know you are, what's the point of discussing it? But since you ask, it probably wouldn't make any difference. With your looks, you'd be a model or something equally frivolous. Your response just now proves it. One harmless kiss and you expect it to mean something.'

'You can't condemn me for having feelings,' she protested, feeling increasingly infuriated with him. What did he think she was made of—stone?

'No, but there's a time and place for everything,' he returned in clipped tones. He glanced at his watch. 'We'd better be going, Pixie's expecting us.'

They accomplished the drive to Stawell in stony silence. The rattling of the utility and the crunch of gravel beneath the wheels before they turned on to the main road would have made talking difficult in any case, but after this morning she didn't care if they never spoke to each other again.

He was the most horrible, insensitive man she had ever met. Of course, she should have known he couldn't change that much. Only an insensitive brute would have made fun of a thirteen-year-old he found cramming herself with cakes under a table, while everyone else was socialising. He had called her a greedy pig, without knowing that food was her only consolation during the stormy last days of her parents' marriage. Fortunately, Aunt Pixie had enabled her to see that this course was only hurting herself. A man like Talan would never understand such human failings.

'You'll have to do better than this when we get to the hospital,' he said as they entered the outskirts of the town.

'Don't worry, I know how to behave—darling,' she said with all the sarcasm she could muster.

As he helped her out of the car in the hospital car-park, he glanced at her left hand. 'At least you remembered the ring.'

'Care to put it through my nose?' she shot back angrily but he had already turned away and was striding towards the main building, leaving her no option but to trot after him.

When they were shown into the intensive care ward where Pixie was, she forgot everything else but how much she loved her aunt, enough to slip her hand convincingly through Talan's and stand close to him at her aunt's bedside.

Pixie Pride was a striking woman whose personality made one forget her doll-like proportions. Even lying in bed, she held herself elegantly and her black hair was neatly combed back from a centre parting into a knot at her nape. All the same, Joselin was shocked by the change in Pixie's appearance. Her skin was waxen and tightly drawn over her bones, giving her a skeletal look, and her breath came in difficult gasps. When speaking, she had to pause after each few words to catch her breath.

'Why didn't you tell me you were ill?' Joselin chided gently.

'I didn't want to worry you, dear.'

Since Joselin had held back the details of her own ordeal for the same reason, she smiled in understanding. 'Well, I'm glad I know now, so we can take care of you,' she said firmly.

Pixie shook her head. 'You'll have enough to do taking care of each other. I'm so glad you two have fallen in love—although you were wicked to keep me in suspense.'

'That's precisely why we did it,' Talan intervened. 'We didn't need a matchmaker.'

The old lady chuckled. 'I can see that. Maybe you'll

stop all this film business now that you have Talan to consider, Joselin.'

She shot him an anxious look but Pixie didn't elaborate, leaving Talan's impression that she was an actress intact. 'We'll see, Aunt Pixie. We aren't making any plans until you have your operation.'

Talan coughed significantly. 'When are you going to have it, Pixie, now that Joselin is here to take care of me?'

'The doctor wants me to have it right away, but I've persuaded him to let me wait until after the ceremony.'

Joselin and Talan exchanged worried looks, hastily redirected towards Pixie. 'The ceremony?' Talan asked for both of them.

'Oh, I hope you won't mind getting married in a hospital room. The doctor won't let me get out of bed even for that, but he says it's all right if you two come here. Then if anything goes wrong, at least I'll die happy, after seeing you two safely married.'

They should have anticipated something like this. Desperately, Joselin flashed Talan a look of appeal but he dumbfounded her by saying decisively, 'Of course we don't mind—do we, *darling*?'

Later, as they walked back to the utility, Joselin shook him by the arm. 'How could you agree to such a thing?'

'We have to go through with it. You saw how ill Pixie is. She's a stubborn woman. If we don't have the ceremony she'll go on refusing the operation until it's too late.' His eyes bored into hers like twin flames. 'Besides, is it so hard to countenance— marrying me?'

If she hadn't responded so ardently to his kiss this morning, she would have said no straight away. As it was, her own eagerness bewildered her. Did she want to marry him, even though they knew next to nothing about each other?

Maybe her doctor was right—she did have a subconscious wish to be taken care of, and this was her body's way of ensuring it. If so, she wanted no part of it. Once she recovered from this period of weakness, she would regret her action for the rest of her life. But she was still left with the problem of Pixie.

'All right, I'll do it,' she said with a heavy heart. 'We can always get an annulment as soon as Pixie's well.'

Talan paused in the act of opening the car door for her, and leant against it, regarding her seriously. 'Oh, I doubt that very much.'

'What do you mean? Surely you wouldn't hold me to a marriage under such conditions?'

'No, it wasn't that. I meant I doubt whether we'll be able to get an annulment. A divorce maybe, but . . .'

'Now just a minute,' she intervened. 'If you think I'm going to sleep with you just because we have a bit of paper which says we're married, you're crazy.'

'I don't think we even need the certificate,' he contradicted. 'After the way you responded to a simple kiss this morning, it wouldn't take much persuasion to get you into my bed—married or not.'

'I'm afraid you've just made it impossible for me to go through with this farce,' she said defiantly, forgetting for a moment why they were even discussing it. 'If I can't trust you to behave like a gentleman . . .'

'Who said I was a gentleman?' Even so, he belied his words by opening the car door for her. His fingers grazed her shoulder as she got in, and a charge like an electric current shot through her. Good grief! She couldn't even let him touch her without evoking a response. How could she risk marrying him?

'You don't have any choice, you know,' he reminded

her as they drove through the town, back to the main
road to Yarrakina. 'You saw how ill Pixie is.'

She remained silent, sunk in despair. He was
right—Pixie's life depended on what she did next. And
yet how could she marry him when he had made it
clear he intended to take full advantage of the
situation? 'I'll do it on one condition—that you
promise not to try to claim your . . . your conjugal
rights.'

'And if I won't promise?'

Suddenly she felt the hated tears, always so near the
surface now, spring to her eyes. 'You're despicable,
using a sick woman to get your own way. I'm sure you
aren't short of female company—so why me?'

They travelled quite a bit further before he
answered. 'I'm blowed if I know.'

The answer she most wanted to hear was that he
cared for her, even a little, which would make this
whole thing bearable. But it seemed he wasn't going to
allow her any concessions at all. 'Very well, you win,'
she said heavily. 'I can't let Pixie die and you know it.'

At the same time, a possible way out of the situation
was starting to form in her mind. Anxiously, her
glance flickered to Talan but all his attention was on
steering the car down the rutted side road. In any case,
he couldn't read her mind, so there was no way he
could find out her devious plan in time to thwart her.

As they neared the homestead, they passed some of
the stockmen hooking her sports car up to a larger
towing vehicle. Talan pulled up and spoke to them
through the open window, soon ascertaining that her
car was driveable, having sustained no mechanical
damage. 'Just a few scratches and dents,' he explained
as he leaned back inside and wound the window up.
'Your car will be back at the homestead this
afternoon.'

She was so preoccupied with hatching her little scheme that she'd completely forgotten her car. 'That's good,' she said absently, earning a curious look from Talan.

'What are you up to?' he asked suspiciously.

She flushed, annoyed with herself for displaying such obvious signs of guilt. 'Why should I be up to anything?' she asked a shade too quickly.

'Well, you were so quiet there.'

Here was her opening. 'Actually, I was thinking about the ... that is, our ... wedding. Did you have anyone in mind to perform the ceremony?'

'The local minister, I suppose. I haven't been the most regular church-goer, but Pixie has and I'm sure he'd oblige for her sake.'

She turned side-on to him, composing her features into a look of appeal. 'Then would you mind very much if I called a friend of mine from Melbourne? He's a marriage celebrant.'

'Since you've had so little say in your own wedding so far, I guess that isn't too much to ask,' he said to her amazement. She had expected much more of an argument for some reason. 'OK, go ahead and call him. I'll make all the necessary arrangements and we can have the ceremony at the hospital in a few days time.'

As soon as they were back at the homestead, Talan announced that he was riding out to the back paddock to see how the lamb marking was coming along. 'While I'm gone, you can call your friend in Melbourne,' he suggested.

It was exactly what she planned to do, but she hadn't expected him to make it so easy for her. 'I'll do that,' she said with a show of reluctance.

She waited until the creak of the flyscreen door announced Talan's departure, then she went to the phone in the hall and sat down at the little table to look up Tony's number.

Then she dialled the long distance code and his number, and crossed her fingers, praying that he would be home. Moments later, the phone was answered. 'Tony, it's Joselin Pride,' she said as the pips died away.

'Josie! Great to hear from you. How's country life?'

'I've only been here two days but already I'm much more relaxed, thanks. I don't suppose anyone has missed me yet?'

'You know the film business—easy come, easy go,' he said ruefully. 'I take it this isn't just a social call?'

'You're right. I rang to ask for a favour. You see, I'm getting married in a couple of days and . . .'

His laughter exploded down the line. 'You? Married! That sure was fast work.'

'There's a good reason for it,' she said to shortcut the explanations. Only afterwards, she realised she had probably given him the impression it was a shotgun wedding.

'Okay, so what's the favour?'

'We're getting married at my aunt's bedside in the hospital,' she said a little breathlessly, 'and I want you to perform the ceremony for us.'

There was a long pause, then he said worriedly, 'But Josie, I'm not . . .'

Suddenly mindful that there were very few truly private telephone conversations in the Outback, she cut in quickly, 'I know you're not really prepared for this at such short notice, but it would mean so much to me if you'd agree to act for us. I'll explain everything when you get here.'

She could almost hear him puzzling it out. 'All right, then, I think I get the picture. I owe you a few favours anyway, so just tell me when and where.'

Speedily, she gave him directions for getting to Yarrakina. She was just about to ring off when Tony added, 'Oh, there's one more thing, Josie. That insurance agent has been hanging around here again. He wanted to know where you'd gone.'

Tony lived in the flat above hers and knew what she'd been through since the accident. 'What did you tell him?' she asked anxiously.

'What do you think? That you'd gone to Timbuctoo and he was welcome to follow you there.'

In spite of her fear, she laughed. 'You're an angel. I thought he would have given up by now.'

'With the kind of money that's at stake, these guys never give up.'

At this, cold fingers of fear clutched at Joselin's heart, overshadowing her relief that Tony had agreed to come. When she hung up the phone, her hands were shaking.

CHAPTER THREE

JOSELIN'S breath caught in her throat as she walked into Pixie's hospital room. It had been transformed into a wedding chapel which someone—the nurses presumably—had draped with white bunting and posies of flowers.

'Like it?' Pixie asked breathlessly.

'It's lovely,' Joselin agreed.

'And so are you, my dear.' Her aunt opened her arms and Joselin went into them, hoping that Pixie would put her fast-beating heart down to wedding nerves.

Talan stood to one side and she avoided catching his eye, but in her first sweeping glance around the room she'd seen how splendid he looked in a classic double-breasted wool suit, which emphasised the breadth of his shoulders and the lean contours of his body.

She knew she looked her best. Her dress was chosen as much to give her the nerve to go through with this, as to please Talan. She wore an organza chemise in white, overlaid with a silver-like paisley embroidery pattern, teamed with the simplest white accessories. It was probably the most feminine outfit she owned and she thanked her lucky stars that her flatmate had talked her into buying it before she left Melbourne. 'For your Academy Award performance someday,' Julie had said. How right she was!

As Joselin straightened from kissing Pixie, Tony Briar came into the room. She'd been shaking with nerves when she introduced him to Talan this

morning, breathing a little easier when the two men
seemed to take a liking to each other.

'Where are the witnesses?' Tony asked.

'Pixie and her doctor have volunteered for that,'
Talan explained. 'He'll be here in a few minutes.'

On cue, Dr Hastings came in, explaining that he'd
been delayed by a minor emergency. The doctor
chuckled. 'We don't often get called to a wedding in
the hospital. In fact, it's so unusual that I took the
liberty of phoning the local newspaper. They've sent a
photographer—I hope you don't mind. The publicity
will help our fund-raising efforts.'

When the photographer walked in, Joselin hoped
her shock was disguised by her careful make-up. This
was a complication she could do without. Tony caught
her eye and lifted an eyebrow quizzically. Helplessly,
she shrugged back.

In any case, there was no time to argue the point
because Tony began assembling the group into a
wedding party, motioning them all to take their places.

Opening a leather-bound folio, he began to read the
familiar words of the wedding ceremony to them.
When he reached the part where Joselin was to make
her vow, he gave her a broad wink. Anxiously, she
glanced at Talan, but he didn't seem to have noticed.

'I will,' she said firmly.

Then Talan slipped a ring on her finger and it was
over. The ring felt cold and strange on her hand. But
there was nothing cold about the kiss he bestowed on
her when instructed to do so by Tony. It was long and
leisurely, reminding her if she needed it, that he could
stir her emotions with uncanny skill.

The organza began to prickle her skin as a sensation
of warmth surged through her, and a hard knot of
feeling twisted in the pit of her stomach. When he
lifted his head, their eyes met and she was disturbed

by his penetrating look. He knew perfectly well what he did to her when he held her, and his look warned her that it wouldn't stop there.

To escape those all-knowing eyes, she turned her attention to Pixie. 'You're crying! This is supposed to be a happy occasion.'

'I'm crying because I'm happy. I never thought I'd see the day when my two favourite people would be married.'

Talan stepped to the bedside. 'Well, now you have, so maybe now you'll sign the doctor's consent form.'

Pixie smiled at Dr Hastings. 'Of course I will, so stop fussing. You two go and have yourselves a honeymoon. I don't want to see you back here for several days.'

Talan laughed. 'Don't worry, Pixie. I'll make sure Joselin doesn't regret today.'

Now what did he mean by that? She flinched as a flashbulb exploded in the room, encompassing them all. 'Last one, folks,' the newspaper photographer assured them. She had hardly been conscious of his activities during the ceremony, but now she was glad to see him go. With any luck, the paper would never use the pictures anyway. Surely there were many more important stories demanding space.

Then Tony produced a marriage certificate for the couple and their witnesses to sign. 'See, I thought of everything,' he whispered to Joselin as she signed her own name, ostensibly for the last time.

She silenced him with a warning glance, anxious to be away from here before Talan decided to ask any awkward questions. Pixie provided her with the perfect exit line. 'Now get out of here, you two.' She looked indulgently up at her doctor. 'I have a date with this handsome young man here.'

As they made their way outside, they were surprised

by a group of nurses who showered them with confetti. 'Good luck!' they chorused, throwing the last of the multi-coloured fragments.

Laughing self-consciously, Joselin thanked them. 'Who's idea was that?' she asked Talan, brushing confetti out of her hair.

'Their own, I expect. As Dr Hastings said, they don't often have weddings here.' He turned to Tony Briar who was following them outside. 'Would you care to join us for a meal? Under the circumstances, there's no reception but it's the least we can do.'

Tony shook his head. 'Thanks, but I have to be on my way back to Melbourne.' He looked significantly at Joselin. 'You know how it is with us marriage celebrants—one lot of vows after another.'

'Flippant character, isn't he?' Talan observed after Tony left them to find his own car.

'Maybe the novelty of the occasion affected him, too.' All the same, she wished that Tony had kept his comments to himself. She could hardly blame him for making light of the occasion, though. He probably thought it was all a great joke. Her main worry now was how Talan would react when he found out that Tony Briar was only an actor with no right to perform marriages. The ceremony was really an elaborate charade to mollify Pixie without committing Joselin to a loveless marriage. She and Talan weren't legally married at all.

On this occasion, the utility had been left behind, replaced by Talan's sleek silver-grey Mercedes and he opened the passenger door for her with great ceremony. 'Thank you,' she mumbled, climbing in.

'What's happened to the radiant bride?' Talan asked, joining her on the driver's side.

'I was never radiant. This marriage was arranged

purely to satisfy Pixie so she'd have her operation, in case you'd forgotten.'

'I hadn't forgotten, but from the way you kissed me in there, I wondered if you had.'

Damn him for being so perceptive. 'I can't help a purely physical response,' she said tartly. 'I'm not a nun, you know.'

'But you *are* dressed in virginal white.'

'This happened to be the only dress I brought with me which was suitable.'

'So you aren't a virgin?'

She felt herself growing hot again. 'I didn't say that, either. In any case, it's none of your business.'

'Oh, but it is my business now. I'm your husband, remember?'

It was on the tip of her tongue to snap that he was no such thing, but she dared not confess just yet. She owed it to Pixie to play out the charade at least until the operation was over. Their arrangement hadn't included a wedding night, whatever he expected.

She had reckoned without the rest of the staff at Yarrakina who were determined to make the most of the occasion. As they drove up to the homestead, she stared in amazement at the giant 'good luck' banner strung across the driveway. 'What's going on here?' she breathed.

'Like the nurses, they're expressing their joy at our happy union,' he said sarcastically. 'Try to look pleased about it, for their sakes if not your own.'

She tried to oblige by fixing a plastic smile to her lips and accepting the flowers the stockmen offered with good grace. 'They're lovely,' she said sincerely. They must have taken up a collection to buy the bouquet for her.

As she started to walk into the house, Talan put a hand on her arm and she realised that the stockmen were still lined up, apparently waiting for something. 'They expect me to carry you over the threshhold.'

She coloured with embarrassment. 'Surely there's no need.'

But before she could protest further, he had scooped her up, bouquet and all, and carried her into the house to the applause and gentle catcalls of the staff. Held tight against him, she felt like a fool, yet from somewhere deep inside, part of her revelled in being pressed against his muscular chest, feeling one hand cradling her legs intimately while his other hand was round her shoulders.

He carried her all the way to the living room before he set her down. Here, the housekeeper, Lillian and a teenager who must be her daughter, Jean, waited for them.

'Good luck to you both,' Lillian said, handing over a large gift-wrapped package.

'No, please you mustn't,' Joselin said, really anxious now. She hadn't counted on involving so many people in her charade. But Lillian insisted she accept the gift and open it there and then. Inside was a hand-carved wooden rocking chair, large enough for a very small child.

'My husband, Bart, carved it,' Lillian explained. 'We were going to buy you something for yourselves, but you already have a well-equipped household, so we thought you could save this for your firstborn.'

Aware that Talan was watching her with that infuriating expression of amusement on his face, she set the rocker down. 'It's very beautiful. Thank you.'

Talan came up behind her and slipped a possessive arm around her waist. 'I'm sure our first child will have a ton of fun with it, won't he, darling?'

With typical male chauvinism, he was already counting on a son, she thought sourly, then her colour heightened as she realised what she was thinking. If a child ever did use the chair, it was unlikely to be her offspring. 'We'll see,' she said non-committally.

'I can see we're embarrassing you,' Lillian interrupted. 'Jean and I have prepared a special dinner for you—it's all in the oven so you just have to help yourselves. Don't worry about the clearing up. Leave everything in the sink and we'll take care of it in the morning. Come along, Jean.'

The daughter, who hadn't said a word so far, suddenly came to life and planted a kiss on Talan's cheek, then hugged Joselin. 'Seeing you two makes me long for my own wedding,' she whispered.

'Is she getting married?' Joselin asked Talan after the mother and daughter had left.

'She has a boyfriend over at the neighbouring property, but I think it's mostly daydreams at this stage. Let's not talk about other people tonight. This is supposed to be our night.'

A shadow darkened her face. If only she could tell him the truth, but she dared not in case it somehow got back to Pixie. 'It isn't really our night, you know. I mean, it's not as if we were marrying for love.'

'Love has been known to grow. Look at all the arranged marriages which ended up lasting for decades.'

He sounded as if he wished it could happen to them, which was absurd. He didn't even like her, seeing her purely as a handy way out of Pixie's dilemma. He would probably have made the same proposition to any woman who turned up at Yarrakina at the same time. 'Surely you don't expect me to fall in love with you?' she asked wearily.

'Not in love . . . but to love,' he corrected.

So that was it. Having cornered her, he intended to make the most of her presence to satisfy his male desires. A shudder tore through her at the thought. What would it be like to be made love to by a man like Talan Devereaux?

Well, she wasn't about to find out, she reminded herself sternly. Even though he'd warned her that he expected her to play the part of his wife to the hilt, she had no intention of obeying. Her choice of a virginal white dress wasn't entirely accidental. In a way, it represented the way she felt about sex before marriage. Except that he believed they *were* married, she thought miserably. She should have thought of a way around this problem sooner. Now she was alone in the house with him and it was too late.

He watched the confused play of emotions on her face for a moment then relented. 'Relax, Joselin. You wouldn't be the first bride to have wedding-night nerves. After a few glasses of champagne, everything will seen different.'

Forewarned, she took only sips of the sparkling liquid he splashed into her glass. Since there was no avoiding it, she joined him in a toast to their future, but took the first opportunity to empty her glass into a handy pot plant.

He eyed the empty glass quizzically. 'Hey, slow down! I meant the wine to help you relax, not get you drunk enough to pass out on me.'

Which gave her an idea.

She held out her glass to him. 'Is there any more?'

Frowning, he refilled her glass and watched as she began to sip it. The moment he turned away, she flicked the contents into the hapless pot plant. She was enough of an actress to pretend to be drunk, which would solve her problems for tonight at least.

Dinner provided a further diversion. Lillian had excelled herself by preparing a piquant lemon pepper steak with a crisp spinach and bacon salad. For dessert there was a freshly made strawberry sponge roll. Throughout the meal, Joselin made a show of downing several more glasses of champage, allowing herself to giggle slightly every now and then, while Talan eyed her with disapproval. So he didn't like women who drank too much? Well that was another weapon she could use to keep them apart tonight.

'Don't you think you've had enough?' he asked coldly, as she held out her glass yet again.

'S'lovely. I do like champage,' she said in a forced little-girl voice. 'Don't you?'

'In moderation, the way I like most things.'

'Except women?'

He moved the champagne further away from her. 'Look who's talking. I saw you whispering so cosily with that marriage celebrant, what's-his-name? Tony Briar.'

'So what. I've known Tony a long time,' she said, remembering to slur her words a little.

His eyes narrowed. 'Yet you couldn't resist bringing him along to watch you marry another man.'

'It isn't like that. Tony's a good friend. I got him his break in film acting, so he owes me a favour.'

'I see.'

She forced another giggle. 'You're jealous!'

Proving her point, he slammed his cutlery down on the table. 'Look, this may be an unnatural situation, but couldn't we make the best of it?'

'Make the most of it, don't you mean?'

Immediately, she regretted baiting him because his eyes flashed with a dangerous warning fire. With pantherlike grace, he padded around to her side of the table. 'Since you seem determined to think the worst of me, I might as well do something to deserve it.'

To her dismay, he pushed her, chair and all, around to face him then pulled her to her feet, his grip on her arms irresistible. The small amount of champagne she had actually drunk made her sway against him and his arms tightened around her. 'Why won't you admit that you want me as much as I want you?'

'I . . . I don't! I don't even like you.'

He laughed throatily. 'Still holding that Christmas party against me? My, you do hold a grudge for a long time.'

'Well, you were rotten to me. I'll never forget it.'

'Yet you responded to me before like a long-lost lover.'

All pretence of being drunk was abandoned as she willed her heart to slow its frantic beating. He held her so close that he must feel it pounding against his chest. 'You flatter yourself,' she ground out.

His mouth was so close to her face that she felt the soft wind of his breath ruffling her hair. 'Do I? Then why is every nerve in you begging me to kiss you again?'

He *could* feel her heart racing. His thumb, stroking the inside of her wrist, must have been measuring her pulse as well, which was throbbing so wildly she could hear her own blood singing in her ears. The worst of it was, she did want him to kiss her and it mortified her that he knew it. She decided to try another approach. 'So kiss me. It won't be the first time, nor the last that I've had a few drinks and ended up in a man's arms.'

His mouth inched closer, his teeth gleaming whitely between the full, cynically curving lips. She licked her own lips nervously. 'Liar,' he breathed. 'I'll bet you could count on one hand the number of kisses you've had—and I don't mean the peck-on-the-cheek variety. Why else are you quivering like a captured bird?'

If he didn't kiss her soon and be done with it, she would faint, she just knew it. Her senses couldn't take much more of this overload. 'Why are you doing this to me?' she whispered.

'Because, despite your first impression of me as some sort of rapist, I wouldn't make love to a woman against her will. And I want to make love to you very much, so I have to make you admit that you want me to.'

She shook her head violently, her hair whipping across his face. 'I'll never admit that.'

He blew the strands of hair away. 'Oh no?' Then he closed the small remaining gap between them and claimed her mouth in a soft, searching caress of a kiss which took her breath away.

While her reeling senses absorbed the impact, his hands moved from her wrists to her back, sliding the zipper down below her waist so he could caress her satin skin. As his hands slid inside her dress, she moaned softly and her lips parted instinctively, encouraging him to deepen the kiss. Her body seemed to be acting independently of her will, thrusting wantonly against him. Only then, she realised that he was more than ready to make love to her, and she tried to twist free.

His hold tightened. 'Oh no, you don't. You've just given me the answer I was seeking.'

'No, I . . . I wasn't . . . oh!' The gasp was torn from her as he tugged the organza down over her shoulders so she stood before him in only her flimsy satin bra, the dress dangling around her hips.

'My God, you're beautiful,' he breathed, his eyes clouding with unmistakable desire. 'My beautiful wife.'

Still holding her close, he unhooked the front fastening of her bra so her breasts sprang free of the fabric. Before she could anticipate him, he dropped to his knees and began to shower her upper body with kisses which sent surges of fiery feeling to every part of her. 'Please, Talan, don't,' she moaned, even as part of her cried out for him to continue.

Of their own accord, her hands cupped the sides of his head and guided his questing mouth to each breast in turn. He was right. She wanted him as she had never wanted a man in her life.

Sensing the nearness of her surrender, he pulled her to her knees in front of him. 'Say it, Joselin. Tell me you want me and our wedding night will be a dream come true for both of us.'

In an agony of indecision, she closed her eyes. She would have to tell him the truth. He thought he was making love to his wife, as was his right. What excuse did she have?

'Talan, there's something you should know . . .' she began unhappily.

'Yes, my darling?'

Before she could go on, the telephone shrilled through the house, startling her. She looked at it in dismay, than back to Talan.

'Ignore it,' he urged. 'It's probably only well-wishers anyway. What were you going to tell me?'

A sudden premonition gripped her. 'What if it's the hospital?'

With a curse, Talan got to his feet and went to the phone. He listened for a few minutes then made a curt response which she didn't catch. She made the most of the respite to stand up and fasten her clothing around herself again, although the material felt hot and uncomfortable against her quivering skin. When he returned, she was at least outwardly in command of herself. 'Was it the hospital?'

He nodded. 'Dr Hastings sent a message that Pixie's been rushed into emergency surgery.'

Her hand flew to her mouth. 'Oh, Talan! Will she make it?'

'They think so, but it will be touch and go for a few hours. Do you want to go back to the hospital?'

He had read her mind. 'Please? I couldn't bear it if I stayed here and she . . . she . . .' She couldn't go on.

His arm went around her shoulders but it was a comforting embrace with none of the fiery sensuality of a few moments ago. 'She isn't going to die,' he said firmly. 'Now you go and get your things and I'll get the car out.'

'I'd like to change first. It'll only take a minute.' He nodded and she flew upstairs to her bedroom, averting her eyes from the double bed where they could so easily have been making love at this very minute. She must have been out of her mind to let things go so far! If it hadn't been for the telephone . . .

Pushing such thoughts from her mind, she stripped off her wedding dress and stockings, kicking her shoes across the room. Minutes later she joined Talan outside, wearing grey drill pants tucked into knee boots, with a white silk shirt and grey bomber jacket. Even though it was spring, the nights could still be cool in the Wimmera, and they were likely to be at the hospital for most of the night.

'I put a few overnight things in this bag,' she said, handing a hold-all to Talan who was already in the driver's seat. 'In case we have to be out all night,' she added in case he got the wrong idea. Luckily, in the moonlight, he couldn't see the rush of colour which came to her face at the thought.

His thoughts were too focused on Pixie to misinterpret her intentions. 'Good thinking,' he said tersely and gunned the motor.

For the second time in twenty-four hours, they made the long drive back to Stawell. Although it was the nearest sizeable town to Yarrakina, it was still over an hour's drive, first along unmade roads, then on sealed highway.

Talan drove fast but watchfully. Remembering her recent encounter with the kangeroo, Joselin was glad. They saw a number of the grey shapes bounding along trampoline-fashion beside the road, but none of them ventured on to the road.

It was the first time that Joselin had driven these roads by moonlight since her teens. Despite her anxiety over Pixie, she stared around in wonder, absorbing the sheer beauty and tranquillity of the nightscape. The river red gums, so stark by day, became things of beauty when silvered by moonlight. The merino sheep were just blobs of grey in the paddocks, calling attention to themselves only by the occasional plaintive bleat.

Again and again, her eye was drawn to the distant outlines of the Grampians, each rocky outcrop clearly silhouetted against the night sky. Occasionally a black shape flew overhead—owls, she knew—but suggesting Dracula on the wing, the fantasy heightened by the thrup-thrup of the broad wings in the still air.

Momentarily, Talan's hand left the steering wheel and clasped hers in her lap. 'She'll be all right,' he repeated.

'I know. I wasn't worrying, really. I was just appreciating . . . all this.' Words failed her.

'I know. I feel the same way about the place. That's why I was so determined to buy a property here. I didn't think a girl like you would appreciate it, though. I mean . . . coming from the bright lights of the film world and all.'

'I just work in the film industry. It doesn't stop me appreciating other things,' she said stiffly. She had forgotten that he still thought she was an actress. It was another untruth which would have to be cleared up between them soon.

He interrupted her thoughts. 'What were you going to tell me, before the phone rang?'

Recalling the warmth of his arms and what had so nearly happened, she shivered. 'It ... it's not important now.' And it wasn't. Now that her aunt was having her operation, there was no need for them to keep up the pretence of their marriage any longer. As soon as they knew that Pixie was all right, they could go their separate ways, so there was no need for a big confession scene. What she had to tell him could more easily be put into a letter after she was long gone from here. He would probably be relieved to find he wasn't burdened with her after all. She was astonished at the pain this thought caused her.

He shrugged and concentrated on his driving. They stopped only once, to have coffee at a roadside cafe, then drove straight on to Stawell, which was dark and silent, most people having gone to bed for the night.

Driving through the streets, they passed the illuminated fountain going through its cycle of colour changes, presided over by the marble warrior atop the war memorial. Shortly afterwards they pulled up outside the red brick hospital building.

'You go inside and wait while I park the car,' he instructed.

Needing no second invitation, she hurried inside and was directed to a waiting room near the operating theatre. A nurse came out and spoke briefly with her, but could only tell her that the operation was progressing as expected. So far, Pixie was holding her own. 'There's nothing more I can tell you,' she apologised.

'Is it all right if we wait till it's over?'

The nurse smiled understandingly. 'Of course. There's a coffee machine in the corner, but I warn you, it could be a long wait.'

Forewarned, Joselin made herself as comfortable as she could on the vinyl upholstered couch in the waiting room. It was warm in the room so she shrugged off her jacket, mindful that she might need its warmth when she went outside again later. Soon afterwards, Talan joined her there. 'Any news?'

'She's holding her own, that's all they'll say. It seems the excitement of the ceremony this morning was too much for her heart to take. She collapsed earlier this evening and they decided not to wait any longer.'

His face was bleak with self-condemnation. 'I should have put my foot down when she suggested having the ceremony here.

Her heart went out to him and she rested a hand on his arm. 'We're both to blame in that case, but the doctor said it was all right.'

'All the same . . .'

'Don't, please,' she begged, her voice tight with unshed tears. 'It's too late to change anything now.'

He squeezed her hand tightly. 'I'm sorry, I know you feel as badly about this as I do. But you're right, we couldn't have known what would happen.' He dropped down on to the couch beside her. 'This isn't much of a wedding night for you, is it?'

'For you neither.'

He grinned ruefully. 'Don't I know it? Right now, I planned to be alone with you at Yarrakina, the two of us together in my king-sized bed.'

'It's called counting your chickens,' she said sourly, unwilling to be reminded of how close his plans had come to fruition.

'You can't deny you were ready,' he argued.

'I wasn't denying it. But it was a purely physical reaction which you did everything in your power to provoke. You seem to have forgotten why we arranged this so-called marriage in the first place.'

'Oh, I hadn't forgotten. But I wonder if Pixie's illness was the only thing which made you agree to marry me.'

'Of course it was. What other reason is there?'

'A very strong attraction which exists between us and which is very, very mutual.'

She averted her gaze from him. 'That's absurd. We hardly know each other.'

'I've known you since you were a little girl, remember?'

'But that was different. You made it very clear that you thought I was a nuisance then. And you've made it quite clear that you have no time for women like me now.'

He shook his head. 'I said I have no time for women who use their wiles to get their own way. You haven't shown any signs of doing that so far.'

If he only knew! By inviting Tony to perform their 'wedding' ceremony, she had been more devious than he knew. 'Next thing, you'll be saying that you wanted to marry me all along,' she said in exasperation.

'That's exactly what I am saying. But I couldn't very well say that to a thirteen year-old girl, now could I?'

Could he possibly have seen in the child she'd been, the seeds of the woman he wanted to marry? 'That's nonsense,' she said dismissively. 'You don't have to justify your actions to me, you know. I'm quite happy to accept that you asked me to marry you purely to help Pixie.'

He tilted her chin so she was forced to meet his eyes. 'Are you, Joselin? Are you quite sure that's the only reason you agreed?'

She tried to pull free but was held in an iron grip. 'Let go, you're hurting me,' she protested.

'Just trying to get at the truth. This evening, I made

you admit that you wanted me to make love to you. Why won't you admit you wanted to marry me for your own reasons as well?'

This time, she managed to jerk free and backed to the furthest limit of the couch. Had she agreed to marry him purely out of love for Pixie, or was there something deeper involved? She had always believed she disliked him for neglecting her so much when they stayed at Yarrakina together. When he had teased her about eating the cream cakes, her dislike had been fuelled into active hatred. But wasn't hatred the other side of a coin called love? Maybe she'd resented his neglect so much because she badly wanted him to notice her. She'd been unable to alter the gap in their ages, so she could have turned her frustration into dislike for him. Why hadn't she considered that before?

She shifted uncomfortably in her seat. She couldn't very well confess that he might be right, or he would think she was ready to carry on where they'd left off this evening. Nor could she let him treat her as his wife without telling him the truth. Once he knew how she'd deceived him, he would dismiss her as one of those women he despised, who schemed and connived to get their own way. It was a hopeless dilemma.

'So you aren't going to admit it,' he said heavily. 'It seems I'll have to find a way to make you.'

He leaned towards her and she glanced around the room, seeking some way of escape but the corridors remained deserted. 'Since you can't very well rape me here in the hospital, I don't have to admit anything,' she said desperately.

His expression turned cold. 'It was hardly rape before. You were willing enough, in fact you were practically begging me to make love to you.'

'Do you have to be so crude?'

'So, it's crude now, is it? I don't know what to make

of you, Joselin. One minute, you're all compliant and sexy as hell, the next prickly and touch-me-not.'

With an exasperated sigh, he got up and strode to the coffee machine, making a cup for each of them. Wordlessly, she accepted the one he handed to her, although she didn't really want to drink it. It was something to do to avoid talking to him any more.

She'd been an idiot not to recognise what was really going on, she could see that now. She had told herself she was acting nobly, to help Pixie, but she was really pleasing herself all along. She had wanted Talan, she admitted it now, but she had been so afraid of his rejection—having experienced it so often as a child— that she had staged the fake ceremony as a kind of self-protection.

In reality, she had probably spoiled her one chance of gaining his love.

The silence between them grew deafening, but the more she searched for the words which would heal the breach between them, the more they eluded her. He remained standing with his back to her, staring moodily out at the night.

When she thought she couldn't take another minute of his accusatory silence, the swing doors leading to the operating theatre opened and two men came out in surgical caps and gowns, their masks dangling around their necks. One of them she recognised as Dr Hastings.

Her heart began to thud in her breast as she and Talan turned simultaneously, enjoying ironically, the first unity of the last few hours. 'How is she?' he asked for them both.

The doctor's tired face relaxed into a smile. 'She's fine. Still in a critical condition, I'm afraid, but the surgery was a complete success. If she handles the next few hours okay, she'll make a complete recovery.'

Joselin's eyes were shining and as she turned to
Talan, she saw that he had moisture on his cheeks.
'Thank God,' she breathed. 'When will we be able to
see her?'

'Not for some time yet, I'm afraid. But there's no
point in your waiting here any longer. Why don't you
get a room in town for what's left of the night, and
come back in the afternoon when you can see her?'

Spend the night in a hotel room alone with Talan?
Her blood cooled at the very idea, but she had
reckoned without the barriers she'd erected between
them tonight. 'We'll do that,' he said coldly, not
looking at her. Somehow she knew she would have
nothing to fear from him tonight, if fear was the right
word.

The other surgeon bid them good night and went
back through the swing doors, but Dr Hastings
hesitated. 'There's nothing wrong between you two, is
there?'

Talan's face was a study in indifference. 'What
makes you ask that?'

'Well, I know how much your marriage means to
Pixie. If there's anything wrong, I wouldn't advise
sharing it with her until she's completely well.'

Joselin stifled a gasp. Her plan to slip away as soon
as possible, leaving a note for Talan, collapsed into
dust. She would have to remain here as his wife until
Pixie was well enough to be told the truth.

Talan took her elbow and steered her towards the
corridor. 'Don't worry, doctor. *My wife and I* won't
do anything to hinder Pixie's recovery, will we,
darling?'

'N . . . no, of course not.' What else could she say,
knowing that her compliance was vital to save Pixie?
What she couldn't help wondering as Talan escorted
her back to the car was—who was going to save her?

CHAPTER FOUR

THEY drove to a motel on the Western Highway where, luckily, Talan knew the owner well enough to disturb her at such a late hour. When she saw who it was, she was only too happy to let them have a room until lunchtime the next day.

'You're lucky, it's the last vacancy,' Mrs Stokes explained as she led them to their room.

As they walked, Joselin stumbled a little from tiredness and was grateful for the hand Talan put under her elbow. Mrs Stokes showed them into the room then bid them good night and closed the door behind herself.

It was a modern motel suite with deep green shag carpeting, floor-to-ceiling windows now covered by heavy curtains in a paler green, and a well-equipped bathroom opening off it on the right. To Joselin's tired eyes, however, the most welcome sight was of two neat single beds separated by a white lacquered chest of drawers. At least she would have no problems with Talan tonight.

He followed the direction of her gaze. 'Sorry about this, but I couldn't very well insist on a double.'

If he only knew how thankful she was for the single beds! 'That's all right. I'm so tired all I want to do is fall into bed and go straight to sleep.'

'All the same it wasn't what I had in mind for our wedding night.'

She glanced at her watch. 'Our wedding night ended an hour ago.'

'Yes, but not in the way I meant.'

She knew perfectly well what he meant but she wasn't about to let him get close to her again until she'd had a chance to explain about the ceremony. Yet she couldn't until the doctor assured them that Pixie was out of danger. It was going to take all her imagination to stay out of his bed until then.

Rummaging through the overnight bag, she found her toilet things and headed for the bathroom. Before going under the shower, she checked that the bolt on the door was secure. Talan might well be tired but there was no point in provoking him unnecessarily.

The hot shower felt wonderful and she stayed under it a long time, then rinsed her underwear in the basin. If she draped it over the central heating unit, her bra and paints would be dry enough to put on again when she awoke. With no dressing gown to put on, she swathed herself in one of the motel's bath sheets. Then she gathered her newly washed clothes and took them back into the room with her.

She needn't have worried about provoking Talan with her skimpy attire. When she emerged from the bathroom he lay stretched out on top of the bedclothes, fully dressed and sound asleep. As she looked down at him, his features composed in sleep, she felt a wave of tenderness wash over her, forgetting for a moment that he wasn't really her husband. His tall frame barely fitted the standard sized bed, and his broad shoulders touched each side of the mattress. What a splendid looking man he was! What would it be like to have him make love to her, as he was about to do when the telephone rang?

Shaking herself mentally, she shed the towel and climbed into the other bed. There was no point even thinking about Talan in that way. Once he found out how she had deceived him, his anger would put an end to any feelings he had for her.

Resignedly, she reached for the bedside lamp and snapped it off. At once, the room was plunged into pitch blackness, the thick curtains shutting out the reassurring moonlight.

She tensed as a film of perspiration formed on her forehead and she clutched the bedclothes tightly. Oh God, she couldn't have a panic attack now, in front of Talan. Desperately, she focused on the even sound of his breathing, loud in the still night air. In . . . out . . . in . . . out . . .

Gradually, as her breathing synchronised with his, she began to relax a little, enough to let her exhaustion overcome her.

Then they were back, hundreds of them—although she couldn't have said what 'they' were. Swooping and diving on her out of the darkness, their bat-wings stirred the air and chilled her face. She screamed at the top of her lungs, but no sound came out.

'Joselin, wake up! You're dreaming!'

Something sharp stung the side of her face and with a shock, she realised Talan had hit her. She opened her eyes to find the room flooded with light from an overhead fitting. Talan sat on the edge of her bed. She clutched the side of her face and stared at him dizzily. 'Why did you do that?'

'You were hysterical. Some sort of nightmare, I gather. Care to tell me what it was all about?'

'I . . . I don't know. It's a . . . a dream I have sometimes. It terrifies me.'

The corners of his mouth arched upwards in a humourless smile. 'So I gather. It terrified me, too, waking up to find you screaming your head off.'

'I'm sorry I woke you,' she apologised stiffly.

'That's okay. You couldn't help it.' He went to where an electric kettle and tea things were set out on a tray, and switched the kettle on. 'You'll feel better after you've had a cup of tea. Then maybe we can both get some sleep.'

'What time is it?'

'Nearly dawn.'

So she'd been asleep for several hours when it had only seemed like minutes. She felt a little better knowing that he'd got a little rest at least.

He brought the tea to her and she took it thankfully, being careful not to let the blanket slip down when she sat up to drink it.

He noticed the movement and smiled. 'No pyjamas?' ·

'There wasn't time to pack properly.'

'Never mind. I never sleep in them anyway.'

To her horror, he returned to his own bed and began to strip off his shirt, tie and trousers. She looked quickly away when he got down to his underpants. 'You could at least get undressed in the bathroom.'

'What for? We are married, so you'd better get used to seeing me like this.'

Unselfconsciously, he stepped out of the underpants and let them drop to the floor. His back was to her and she caught a glimpse of perfectly sculpted hips a shade or two lighter than the dark tanning of his muscular legs. He must swim in the nude sometimes to tan so evenly all over, she thought idly, then blushed furiously. She would have to stop thinking about him like this or she would start believing in their fictitious marriage herself.

Her relief as he slid into his bed was short-lived when he rolled over on to one elbow and looked at her. 'What brought the nightmare on tonight?'

She didn't really want to talk about it, especially not to him. 'It was so dark in here,' she explained unwillingly.

His disgust was thinly veiled. 'Don't tell me you're afraid of the dark?'

'I didn't used to be. Only since . . .'

'Since what?'

'Nothing. I'm just one of those weak women you're always on about.'

'I don't believe you,' he said flatly. 'A weak woman would have broken down while we waited for news of Pixie. You held up like a veteran.'

'That was different.'

'Was it? I don't recall you panicking when your car went into the ditch, either.'

She set the cup down on the bedside table so hard that it rattled in its saucer. 'Stop trying to make me into something I'm not. I'm a . . . a hopeless coward, for one thing. I'm afraid of the dark and it takes all the nerve I've got to get into an enclosed car.' Which was the reason why she'd exchanged her old Mini Minor for an open-topped sports car, but he didn't know that.

He wasn't about to let her off so easily. 'Sounds like you were in a car accident, a pretty bad one. Am I right?'

He was getting uncomfortably close to the truth. 'So what if I was. I don't want to talk about it.'

'It might help.'

'Not to you, it wouldn't.'

'I see.' From the chill in his voice, she knew he was hurt by her dismissal. He rolled over with his back to her, making her long to reach out and touch him, say she was sorry, she didn't mean it the way it sounded.

But she was sure once he knew the full story, he would despise her for her weakness, as she despised herself. It was better if she left things as they were. At least this way she still had his respect, if not his love.

This time, as soon as she turned out the light she

scampered to the window and pulled the curtains a
little apart, allowing the moonlight to flood the room.
Reassured, she was able to fall asleep this time without
any more nightmares.

It was full daylight by the time she next awoke.
Talan's bed was empty and she heard the sound of the
shower running.

Making the most of her opportunity, she jumped
out of bed and rescued her underwear from the
radiator. It was dry enough to put on.

She was fully dressed by the time he came out of the
bathroom, towelling his damp hair. He, too, was
dressed in his shirt and trousers from the previous
day. The jacket of his suit was draped over a nearby
chair. 'Just as well we didn't get married in morning
clothes,' he observed wryly.

As he spoke, there was a knock on the door.
Opening it, Joselin found Mrs Stokes standing there
with a laden tray. 'I left your breakfast as late as I
could but the kitchen staff go off duty at eleven,' she
explained apologetically.

Thanking her, Joselin took the tray from her and
backed into the room with it, setting it down on a
small table under the window. 'There's enough here to
feed an army,' she said, peeping under the insulated
covers.

There was bacon, eggs and crisp fried potatoes,
freshly squeezed orange juice and heaps of hot
buttered toast and marmalade. Seeing it, Talan
chuckled. 'Good old Mrs Stokes.'

He sat down at the table across from her and helped
himself to toast. 'How did you sleep last night? Did
the tea help?'

So he hadn't forgotten the nightmare. 'Yes, it did,
thank you,' she said in a tone meant to discourage
further questioning.

He was not deterred. 'When did you have the accident?'

'I told you, I don't want to talk about it.'

'I see. What if I tell you I owe you an apology?'

'Why should you apologise? I was the one who disturbed your sleep.'

'I didn't mean that. I mean I was rushing things a bit last night. Given the circumstances of our marriage, maybe I ought to give you more time to get used to the idea before we take things any further.'

She stared at him in amazement. 'That wasn't your attitude last night.'

'Last night, I was alone with a beautiful woman who I felt I had every right to take to bed.'

Had he found out about the ceremony? 'Nothing's changed, has it?' she asked carefully.

'I've changed. Dammit, Joselin, I want this to work. I feel we could have something very good together, even if it did start off in a bizarre way. I don't want to blow it by rushing things.'

She could hardly believe her ears. 'You're willing to wait until I'm ready?'

'As long as it takes.'

'But why?'

'Last night, when you were having the nightmare, you screamed in your sleep. You called out my name. That did something to me, Joselin.'

'I don't want your pity,' she ground out. 'I can handle my own problems.'

In the act of pouring juice into their glasses, he froze, then slammed the jug down on to the table. 'It isn't pity, for goodness' sake. Why are you trying so hard to make me dislike you?'

Tears brimmed in her eyes, coming dangerously close to spilling over. 'I just don't want you to get the

wrong idea about me. You don't like me—you don't
even know me.'

'Then let me get to know you. Tell me about
yourself.'

She knew what would happen if she did. His whole
attitude towards her would change. He'd stop trying to
take care of her, as was his instinctive reaction now, and
would expect her to be strong and self-reliant when that
self didn't even exist anymore. It was what the doctor
had cautioned her against. Miserably, she shook her
head. 'I can't explain why, but I . . . I just can't.'

There was an almost tangible atmosphere of
hostility between them as they finished their breakfast.
Talan cleared his plate while she merely picked at her
food. Afterwards, they packed their few belongings,
settled their bill with Mrs Stokes, and drove in
awkward silence back to the hospital.

On the way to Pixie's room, Talan took her arm.
Instantly she stiffened and he made a throaty sound of
impatience. 'I only touched you, for heaven's sake!'

'Then don't,' she snapped back.

'How do you think it will look to Pixie if her loving
couple stand three feet apart? She's bound to guess
that something's wrong.'

He was right. For her aunt's sake she had to make an
effort to look like a radiant bride, at least until Pixie was
well enough to be told the truth. She tried to relax as
Talan tucked her hand in his arm, but the brush of his
body sent shock waves right through her, making her
want to weep with frustration. It took all of her film
training to compose her features into a mask of
happiness which was only marred by concern for her
aunt.

The first sight of Pixie, so petite and frail, drove all
thoughts of herself out of her mind. Her aunt lay in
the high hospital bed, amid a tangle of monitoring

equipment and bottles of liquid feeding into a tube in her arm. Even so, Pixie managed a brave smile as they approached. 'Sorry about the honeymoon,' she whispered.

'Never mind that, think of yourself for once. I . . . we . . . just want you to get well.'

Her aunt's hand fluttered feebly on the bedclothes and Joselin slipped hers into it, feeling the grip tighten. 'At least if anything happens to me I'm glad you've got each other now.'

Frightened, Joselin glanced at Talan. 'Nothing's going to happen to you,' he said firmly. 'The worst is over now. Once you get over the after-effects of the surgery, Dr Hastings tells me you'll be wandering the Grampians again in no time, cataloguing painting sites and no doubt discovering new ones.'

Pixie's eyes began to twinkle and a little colour seeped into her cheeks. Trust Talan to find the right medicine for her! 'Have you told Joselin yet?' she asked.

'Told me what?' Joselin asked as Talan shook his head. 'What's going on between you two?'

'It's a little surprise of mine, sort of a wedding present for you.'

Before Joselin could ask any more, Talan slipped his arm around her shoulders. Although she trembled slightly, she managed to keep from pulling away. 'I'll show her on the way back to Yarrakina,' he promised.

'Show me what?' she persisted after they had left Pixie to rest.

He refused to tell her any more, leaving her to seethe with impatience as they returned to the car. It was as if he knew how tantalised she was by mysteries. When she was a child, her family never dared leave her Christmas presents under the tree because she could never resist peeking at them. Repeated cautions about curiosity and the cat fell on deaf ears. Talan

couldn't have found a better way to ensure her co-
operation on the drive back to the property.

No sooner had they turned off the sealed road on to
the sandy track leading to the homestead, than he
turned off yet again on to a spur road that was no
more than twin tyre tracks between two paddocks.

As they gained height steadily, she realised they
were driving up into the ranges, the birds and
wildflowers becoming more evident the further they
went from civilisation.

Soon, the eucalyptus were alive with screeching
lorikeets and busy honeyeaters darted down to drink
from the flowering plants. Once, she caught a glimpse
of a red deer alongside the road. There was colour
everywhere, from the white of the smoke-bush and
tea-trees to the pink of the heath and begonias, and the
gold of the wattle. Most spectacular of all were the
massed displays of Grampians Thryptomene with
their starry white petals surrounding gold or blood-
red centres.

'Still curious?' Talan asked, never taking his eyes off
the steep, sandy track.

She was gripped by a fever of curiosity but she
wasn't going to give him the satisfaction of admitting
it. 'I'm just enjoying the scenery,' she said airily. 'I'd
forgotten how beautiful it is.'

'I see.'

He seemed annoyed by her refusal to enter into the
spirit of the game. Under different circumstances, she
probably would have been glad to, but she was much
too conscious that he still believed they were married.
She ought to tell him the truth, but she baulked at
destroying his trust in her.

All the same, she couldn't go on enjoying his
attentions under false pretences. No matter what it
cost her, she would have to tell him as soon as they

reached the homestead, after he'd shown her whatever was at the end of this spur.

They left the car in a clearing, laughing at a kangaroo who appointed himself parking attendant. He sat back on powerful hind legs and tail, to keep watch on their vehicle.

'He obviously doesn't trust that kookaburra up there,' Talan observed, pointing to a tree branch where the kingfisher-like bird sat clutching a small tree snack in a beak half the length of its body.

Walking with Talan along a white sand path through the scrub, Joselin felt carefree, as if by severing the ties with civilisation, she had also left behind her fears and problems. If only they could stay like this, so warm and companionable. If only she didn't have to confess and ruin everything.

Talan stopped suddenly, in front of a wall of greenery. 'Here we are.'

'I don't see anything, except the bush.'

He pulled the curtain of creepers to one side and revealed a rock face sheltered by an overhang, similar to other ancient aboriginal painting sites she'd visited around the ranges.

The rock surface was covered with hundreds of stencilled hands—small, childlike hands; large feminine hands; broad masculine ones. They were painted in red ochre pigment over every inch of the rock.

'Impressive, isn't it?' Talan asked when she remained silent, her eyes wide with surprise.

She found her voice with an effort. 'How long have you known this place was here?'

'Pixie discovered it a couple of months ago. We're the only three white people to have seen it in centuries, I'd say. Pixie wanted me to bring you here as a kind of wedding gift from her.'

'It's completely intact and untouched, unlike the

other one,' she said, referring to the so-called Cave of
Hands which had been discovered in the district in
1929. Unlike the other shelter, this one was untouched
by vandals and needed no protective wire screen over
the paintings.

The smile she bestowed on Talan was warm and
genuine. 'What a marvellous present—to share in such
a discovery.' Only then she remembered that it was a
present given under false pretences. She half-turned
away before he could see the shadow which darkened
her eyes.

He would have none of it and clasped her by the
shoulders, turning her back to him. 'What happened
to the smile? I was just starting to enjoy it.'

'I have no right to share this discovery with you.
Pixie only wanted you to bring me here because she
thinks we're married.'

'Well, we are.'

'Not in the way she thinks,' she contradicted. 'Now,
tell him now,' her conscience dictated but courage
failed her and, to her chagrin, she stayed silent.

His hands fell away. 'I'm not sorry about what's
happened, even if you are. Whatever the reason which
brought us together, I'm glad about it. Call it fate if
you like. I think it was meant to be. I would like to try
to make it work. So it's up to you.'

She knew he was waiting for her answer and she had
none to give him. He couldn't know how much she
wanted the union to work—yet she also knew why it
couldn't. Once he found out about the accident and what
it had done to her spirit, he would reject her for her
weakness as he had done when they had been younger.
Rather than take the risk, she had engineered the fake
ceremony. Although she regretted the deception now,
she couldn't alter the situation. It would be another
reason for him to despise her when he found out.

He misunderstood her long silence. 'Look, if it's the sex you're worried about, I told you I don't intend to rush you. I lost my head last night but, dammit, you're a beautiful, desirable woman. You can't blame me for wanting you.'

'I don't blame you for anything,' she said tiredly. 'I just can't accept the situation as easily as you seem able to do.'

He pushed the hair back from his forehead with a jerky movement. 'Why don't you just admit that you can't stand the sight of me, instead of letting me go on hoping?'

Her head came up. 'It isn't like that at all.'

'Then for God's sake, what *is* it like?'

Clasping her arms around her body in an unconsciously defensive posture she leaned in to the rock shelter, as if seeking a haven from his anger. 'I don't know.'

His lip curled into a sneer. 'You don't know. You don't know whether there's a future for us as husband and wife, and you're not even willing to give it a chance. Maybe it's just as well I didn't make love to you last night. At least now I still have a way out.'

'Is that what you want?'

'It's what I have to want, isn't it?'

Suddenly, the Dreamtime ghosts of the long-ago tribespeople who had left their handprints in the shelter came swirling around her and she shivered violently. Even before she'd had a chance to tell him the truth, he had withdrawn his mantle of love from her.

She felt cold and bereft.

She tried to tell herself it was her own fault that he'd turned on her like this. But it didn't make sense that one minute he was asking for her love, then the next he was casting her aside. There must be some

other explanation, but she was too emotionally
overwrought to think of one.

Since he had already started back towards the car,
she stumbled after him along the path, hoping she
wouldn't take a wrong trail and end up lost. Maybe
she should get lost to pay him back.

At the same time, she knew she would never survive
a night alone in the ranges, surrounded by the
Dreamtime ghosts and the eerie stencilled hands. Even
in broad daylight, they reminded her of the nameless
visions of her nightmares.

When the clearing with the utility parked in it came
into sight, she almost sobbed with relief and stumbled
slightly as she went around to the passenger side.
Talan made no move to open the door for her, sitting
in the driver's seat with his face set and stony as the
hills around them.

Does it have to be like this between us?' she asked in
a small voice.

'It seems so. You've made it perfectly clear that you
won't try to make our marriage work so I'm better off
getting out while I still have some pride left. We'll get
the annulment you obviously want as soon as Pixie's
doctor says she's out of danger.'

It wasn't what she wanted at all but there was no
way she could tell him without explaining why she was
being so aloof. 'I'm sorry for the way things have
turned out,' she ventured.

In profile, his expression remained unforgiving.
'I'm sorry, too. But maybe it's for the best.'

What did he mean by that? Was he starting to be
glad she had given him a reprieve? Maybe he'd been
regretting his offer to try to make the marriage work,
even as he made it.

Miserably, she slumped into her corner of the bench
seat and watched the wildflower-studded bush flash

past with none of her earlier appreciation.

It was approaching dinner time when they drove up to the homestead. With a worried look on her face, Lillian came out to meet them. 'There's someone waiting to see you, Mr Devereaux.'

'Who is it?' he asked without much enthusiasm.

'It's Miss Hall from Jilluka. She says she's come to stay for a few days. Her family bought Jilluka from the Grants—you might have known them when you stayed here as a child,' she explained to Joselin.

Talan went inside without a backward glance. He didn't seem very pleased at the prospect of having a neighbour come to stay, she thought. But he was still out of sorts with Joselin. Maybe a stranger would ease some of the tension between them until Pixie was well enough for them to end this charade.

Lillian's husband, Bart Spencer, the head stockman, led a pair of horses into a yard nearby and smiled a greeting at Joselin. 'How's Mrs Pride?'

Glad to have some normal conversation at last, Joselin smiled back. 'The operation was a complete success. She needs lots of rest and no upsets of any kind, but she should make a complete recovery.'

'That's splendid news, isn't it, Lillian?' His wife nodded agreement. 'Pity it spoiled your night, though.'

As Joselin's face flamed, Lillian wagged a finger at him. 'That's enough of that, Bart.' She bent her head close to Joselin's. 'If I were you, I wouldn't let that Miss Hall stay around any longer than she must. I think she fancies Mr Devereaux herself, but if you ask me, he's done a great deal better by marrying you.'

Appalled, Joselin backed away. 'I'm sure she's only come to wish us well,' she said haltingly, unwilling to encourage gossip.

Lillian's lips tightened. 'Maybe . . . and maybe not.'

Joselin was apprehensive when she went inside to meet the neighbour. She was unprepared for Miss Hall's impeccable grooming and careful make-up, which mocked her own dishevelled appearance. 'Joselin, meet Sonia Hall,' Talan said ungraciously. 'She's going to stay with us for a few days while workmen are doing some extensions on the homestead at Jilluka.'

Sonia's green eyes swept over every detail of Joselin's appearance, giving her the uncontrollable feeling that she was mentally putting a price on everything she wore. Her own clothes were obviously expensive and since she was 'Miss' Hall, her father must be well-to-do. 'How do you do,' she said awkwardly.

'Lillian told me about poor Pixie,' Sonia said sweetly. 'How is she?'

'She's improving, although it will take some time. It was kind of you to come over and enquire.'

Sonia's laugh was high and bell-like. 'Oh, that wasn't why I came, although of course I'm glad she's getting better. We're all very fond of the old girl. She's one of the district's characters, after all. But I really couldn't take any more of that dreadful construction work.'

Through the corner of her eye, Joselin saw Talan stiffen at Sonia's reference to Pixie, but he made no comment. Instead, he busied himself mixing drinks for his guest. 'Mineral water for you?' he asked Joselin.

She nodded and saw Sonia's eyebrow arch disdainfully. She didn't feel inclined to explain herself, so accepted the drink graciously, noting that Talan mixed Sonia's drink without asking. She must have been a regular visitor here since he had bought Yarrakina.

Talan dropped into an easy chair opposite the two

women. 'Now, if it isn't charitable concerns, what really brings you to Yarrakina, Sonia?'

Her long lashes fluttered over her cheeks, creating a coquettish effect which Joselin found irritatingly ingenuous. 'There's only one reason why I keep coming here—you, darling.'

Talan's expression remained impassive. 'You may have done so in the past, sweetheart, but you must have heard on the grapevine by now that I'm a married man.'

'I did better than that. I read about it in the local rag. I've even brought a copy to show you—both of you.'

As her gaze encompassed Joselin, sitting uncomfortably beside her, she had the disturbing feeling that Sonia knew the truth about their marriage. She couldn't have said what made her certain but she was.

'I'll be interested to see it,' Talan said idly, not sounding enthusiastic at all.

'Oh, I'm sure you will be,' Sonia enthused. 'I think you've both been so terribly clever in the way you arranged the whole thing.'

Joselin's whole body turned to ice as Talan sat forward. 'Clever—in what way?'

CHAPTER FIVE

SONIA'S body was angled towards Talan but her eyes were fixed on Joselin. 'I only meant it was clever of you to hold the ceremony in the hospital so Pixie could witness it.'

Joselin's breath hissed out between clenched teeth, as Talan said. 'We didn't actually plan it that way. You know she wouldn't go into hospital until she knew I was being well looked after, so we concocted an engagement to stop her worrying. We never dreamed she would go on refusing surgery until we were actually married.'

'So now you poor dears are stuck with each other!'

Joselin flinched but Talan reached for her hand across the chairs. 'Actually, we think it's going to work out pretty well.'

Sonia's eyes widened. 'You don't mean you're going to live here together as if you were really married?'

She knows the truth, Joselin thought miserably. Somehow, Sonia had found out that Tony wasn't really a marriage celebrant and was playing Joselin like a fish on a line. She began to wish she had told Talan the truth herself while they were at the Cave of Hands, but it was too late now.

Fortunately Talan chose to ignore Sonia's last remark and changed the subject. 'You must drive into town and visit Pixie while you're here. She can't have any visitors tomorrow because they're doing some tests, but you can come with us the day after if you like.'

'I'll probably do that,' their visitor said un-enthusiastically and drained her drink.

Joselin decided to follow Talan's lead and keep the conversation on neutral ground. 'How long has your family lived at Jilluka, Miss Hall? I used to go over there regularly when the Grants owned it. I thought after five generations that they'd never sell out.'

'They sold when the price was right, like most people,' Sonia said cynically. 'We bought it about two years ago. Of course, we had to completely raze the house and build something fit for our scale of entertaining.'

Remembering the lovely old sandstone homestead with its honeycomb of high-ceilinged rooms opening off each other, and comfortable wide verandah all round, Joselin felt a pang.

The house had been run-down, she remembered, because the Grants were a large family and there was barely enough money to feed and clothe them all. But it was a shame such a historic property had been destroyed out of hand. She remembered Mrs Grant telling her how the huge oregon beams supporting the house had been brought to the homestead from Melbourne by bullock teams because all workable softwood had to be imported in pioneer days, Australia having little of such timber.

'It's a shame about the house,' she couldn't help murmuring.

Sonia arched one pencilled eyebrow. 'Jilluka is a business as well as a home, Miss Pride. We can't afford to be sentimental about such things.'

What *would* a woman like Sonia be sentimental about, Joselin wondered. Sonia started to chat to Talan about the day-to-day running of their respective sheep stations, completely ignoring Joselin, who was able to gather her thoughts for the first time since Sonia's arrival.

It was obvious that somehow Sonia knew she and

Talan weren't really married. What puzzled Joselin was why she didn't come right out and say it instead of playing cat and mouse like this. She'd made a point of calling Joselin 'Miss Pride', and not 'Mrs Devereaux' as one would expect. Joselin was surprised that Talan hadn't commented on it. It made her wonder if, despite his assertion that he was happy to be married to Joselin, he carried a torch for Sonia Hall.

On her way into the house, Lillian Spencer had warned Joselin that Sonia was interested in Talan—she had already indicated that she was a regular visitor to Yarrakina, and she was certainly treated as one. Why else would she feel free to arrive on Talan's doorstep without warning? The thought left a surprisingly bitter taste in Joselin's mouth.

She drew her attention back to the conversation between Talan and Sonia, and became aware that Talan was watching her, his expression thoughtful.

'So we're shearing the wethers next month, although with all the fuss over these wide-toothed combs, I don't know whether we'll have any shearers to do the job.'

'It's more than a fuss, Sonia. There's been violence at some of the stations where the bosses have insisted on using the wider combs against union opposition.'

Dimly, Joselin recalled that the dispute under discussion was over one type of shearing implement versus another, but there her knowledge ended. She stirred restlessly and Talan picked it up at once.

He stood up and stretched luxuriously. 'I think we'd better go and change. This suit is starting to feel as if it's growing on me.'

He was still wearing his wedding suit. Despite his complaint, it still looked reasonably fresh, the creases standing out crisply against his legs. Joselin knew that her drill jacket and pants hadn't endured as well and she gave him a grateful look. 'Excuse us, please, Sonia. We'll join you for dinner in an hour or so.'

Joselin turned her back on the other woman's expression of annoyance. Perhaps she'd been hoping to bore Joselin into leaving them alone. Joselin wondered how she would spend her time while she and Talan were upstairs.

For a fleeting moment, she wondered if Talan would expect her to share his room with him now but, as she opened her door and went in, he said only, 'See you at dinner.'

Contrarily, she felt disappointed. What had she expected? For him to make good the promise of his comments to Sonia downstairs? It seemed that his pride wouldn't allow him to admit publicly that they were already having problems with their relationship, but nothing had changed between them privately since their harsh words at the Cave of Hands this afternoon.

After their hasty departure yesterday, the room was strewn with clothes, among them her 'wedding' dress. She picked it up and smoothed out the creases. If only she could smooth things out between herself and Talan so easily. Sadly, she hung the dress away in the wardrobe.

Thinking of Sonia's smart green shirtwaister which she must have known set off her auburn hair to great effect, Joselin showered then dressed with more than usual care.

Before going downstairs, she inspected herself critically in the dressing-table mirror, standing up on tiptoe to see all the way to her feet.

Her plans for a relaxing spell in the country hadn't included a honeymoon, so her wardrobe was decidedly casual, but she felt happy with her choice of taupe linen kimono jacket and matching straight-legged trousers over a peach cotton crop top. For a chic touch

she was sure Sonia would notice, she added a peach
floral silk scarf by Oscar de la Renta, which her
flatmate, Julie, had brought back for her from the
USA. Sometimes having a big store fashion buyer for
a flatmate came in handy, she thought.

Why she should be taking so much trouble tonight
she wasn't sure. She only knew she didn't want to
appear drab by comparison with Sonia in front of
Talan. Call it personal pride, she thought, but she
wasn't going to let Miss Hall have everything her own
way.

Why hadn't Talan married *her* instead of Joselin,
she wondered briefly. Sonia was keen enough—it
stuck out a mile. Maybe he would have proposed to
her if Joselin hadn't turned up just when she did.

She bit her lip as she recalled her suspicion that
Sonia was biding her time before revealing everything
she knew. She must want something in exchange for
keeping quiet and Joselin shuddered as she considered
what it might be.

Since she couldn't remain in her room all night, she
slid her feet into black suede pumps and went
downstairs.

Talan and Sonia were already in the dining room,
continuing their discussion of sheep breeding, but
Talan interrupted Sonia long enough to pull out a
chair for Joselin. He had changed into dark brown
chambray jeans and a bronze knitted shirt and her
breathing quickened at the sight of him.

Lillian had prepared seafood cocktails for them,
followed by scallops of veal in a creamy mustard sauce,
with emerald green broccoli and baby new potatoes in
parsley butter.

During the meal, Sonia went out of her way to be
charming and made no further references to the
relationship between Talan and Joselin, although

occasionally, Joselin caught her looking speculatively down the table. What was going on behind those hooded green eyes? Joselin wondered.

They had just helped themselves to the dessert of strawberries and cream when the telephone rang. Frowning, Talan got to his feet. 'I'll answer it.'

'It could be Daddy making sure I got here safely,' trilled Sonia after him. To Joselin she said, 'He worries about me still, you know. He can't seem to get it through his head that I'm twenty-eight now.'

More like thirty, Joselin thought wickedly. Aloud, she said, 'You're lucky to have a parent who worries about you. Most of the time, I don't know where mine are.'

Sonia purred with concern. 'You poor child. Don't you find it difficult having to be so self-reliant at your age?'

At her age indeed! 'How old do you take me for?' she asked a little indignantly.

'Surely you're not long out of your teens?'

'I'm twenty-six as it happens, and I've been fending for myself since I was eighteen.'

Sonia pretended to be hurt. 'No need to be so touchy about it, love. I just wouldn't have taken you for as old as that.'

Or old enough to be serious competition for Talan. That's what she was really saying. Joselin was relieved when Talan came back, although her feelings soon turned to concern when she saw his thunderous expression. 'Who is it? What's the matter?'

'It's for you—your boyfriend, Tony Briar,' he said coldly.

'But I told you he's not . . .'

'Better take it, love,' interrupted Sonia. 'Husbands don't like their wives getting calls from other men.'

Distressed, but with no option but to go, Joselin

hurried out to the hall and picked up the phone. 'Tony?'

'Glad I caught you, Josie. Mr Devereaux didn't sound too pleased to hear from me. He didn't want to put me on to you without telling him what I wanted but I thought you might not want this publicised.'

'What's happened now?' she asked heavily.

'That insurance agent, what's-his-name? He knows where you are and is on his way to see you.'

'But I told him I didn't want anything from his company. I've been telling him that ever since the police caught up with the driver who forced us off the road.'

'His attitude is "that's what they all say". He can't believe that someone who went through what you did wouldn't want to sue for all it was worth.'

Tears sprang to her eyes at the very idea. 'All I want to do is forget the whole thing. Why does he keep pestering me like this?'

Tony was instantly concerned as he heard the distress in her voice. 'Easy, love. You've got a lot of land around you there. Why don't you get the big guy to order him off your land?'

'I . . . I can't,' she said after a pause.

'You mean he wouldn't protect you? What sort of a husband is he . . . I mean, would he be if he was. Heck, you know.'

'I know. And he would protect me, regardless of our real relationship. But he . . . he doesn't know what happened to me. He thinks I'm an actress. My doctor thought I'd have a better chance of getting well if nobody knew who I was or what I did for a living.'

Tony whistled softly down the phone. 'Wow! You've got yourself a real tangle down there, Josie.'

'Don't I know it. Tony, what am I going to do?'

'Well, if you can't tell the big guy the truth, can't

you just tell him this agent is bothering you and get him thrown out anyway?'

She sighed. 'I suppose I'll have to. Thanks for tipping me off anyway.'

'Anytime, love, I just wish I was calling with good news for a change.'

'So do I,' she said as she hung up. 'So do I.'

She braced herself to meet Talan's accusing gaze as she returned to the dining table. 'Well, what did he want?'

'He just wanted to give me some news, nothing important.'

Talan's lip curled into a sneer. 'It can't have been all that trivial or he'd have let me give you a message instead of interrupting our evening.'

Sonia laid a hand on his arm. 'Darling, there are some things a gentleman doesn't ask a lady. Wanting to know about other men's calls is a bit like expecting a girl to kiss and tell.'

Impatiently, Talan freed his arm. 'A man has a right to ask a lady anything he likes if he's married to her.'

Sonia's green eyes swept over Joselin. 'I suppose he does, *if* he's married to her.'

Afterwards, Joselin wondered how she had ever survived an evening of Talan's simmering fury and Sonia's constant innuendos. She was obviously enjoying baiting Joselin, leaving her to wonder just when the bombshell would drop.

In the end, she pleaded tiredness and escaped to her room, no longer caring that she was doing exactly what Sonia wanted her to do. The other woman had been trying to get Talan to herself all evening. Well, she was welcome to him! Joselin thought miserably.

She'd already told him that Tony wasn't a boyfriend, so he had no reason to be suspicious of a simple phone call. And he wouldn't be if she could

only explain why Tony had called. It was her
evasiveness which damned her in Talan's eyes and
there was nothing she could do about it without telling
him the whole sordid story.

In bed, she tossed and turned restlessly, wondering
in spite of herself, what Talan and Sonia were doing
downstairs. In self-defence, she began to get angry.
The fault wasn't all on her side after all. First, Talan
said he wanted her to love him, then he was only too
willing to offer an annulment of their supposed
marriage at the first provocation. How much did Sonia
have to do with that? she mused.

It seemed strange that he was so against manipulative women, yet he was willing to put up with an
expert like Sonia. It was probably just as well the
marriage wasn't real, in that case, she thought angrily,
then wearily admitted that she didn't really believe it
for a minute.

She *did* care, she conceded at last. She would
always care about how Talan Devereaux felt about
her ... for the simple reason that she loved him,
and had done since she was thirteen years old. At
eighteen, he had seemed so attractive. She had tried
to be grown-up and ladylike, so he would notice her
but he never did, being too preoccupied with his
own pursuits. They had drifted apart but she never
overcame her feelings for him. If anything, time and
distance had deepened them. Now, she was hope-
lessly in love with him yet fate had conspired to
deny them a future together.

If only she could have met him a year ago when she
was spiritually whole and strong. There would have
been no need for deception, and their marriage could
have been glorious.

What was the use? The accident had happened,
turning her into a spineless weakling without the

courage even to tell him the truth. What sort of a wife would she be to him as she was now?

Self-pity would get her nowhere, she told herself sternly. She would do better to worry about how to handle the insurance agent if he showed up here. The man frightened her with his persistence. After the accident, he had followed her for weeks, taking photographs of her doing the most ordinary things, and sitting in his car outside her block of flats, where she could see him from a window.

He'd been quite blatant in his activities and laughed when she threatened to call the police. 'All you have to do is sign this disclaimer and I'll go away,' he said, thrusting a form under her nose.

She'd taken it away to read and Tony had been horrified when she told him she intended to sign it. 'You're absolving the insurance company from any future claims concerning your accident,' he told her. 'How can you be sure that some injury attributable to the accident won't surface years from now and prevent you from working? You would need to sue them for compensation then.'

She hadn't thought of it like that. The agent had been furious when she returned the form to the company unsigned, and had renewed his efforts to prove that she was faking her inability to work, in order to extort a large sum of money out of them.

She consoled herself with the thought that he might not be able to locate Yarrakina too easily. It could be days before he got here and by then she would have worked something out.

As she rolled over on her side, the murmur of voices reached her from downstairs. Neither Talan nor Sonia had come up to bed yet. They were still talking when she drifted off to sleep.

Her next awareness was of sunlight streaming into

the room and she sat up, amazed to find the morning
well advanced. She hadn't expected to sleep at all, far
less oversleep.

Fifteen minutes later, dressed in olive green jeans
and a pale green denim shirt with a black velvet tie at
the neck, she went downstairs. Somehow, she knew
that Sonia hadn't given away her secret to Talan yet.
Sonia looked like the sort of woman to enjoy having
her victim on hand when she sprang her trap.

The object of her thoughts was alone in the dining
room when Joselin went in, and she almost backed
away again but it was too late. Sonia looked up and
saw her.

'Good morning!' she trilled.

Joselin managed a small answering smile. 'Good
morning. Where's Talan?'

'He's already had breakfast. He rode out with the
men on a muster hours ago. Said he'd been neglecting
his duties. But we both know why, don't we, *Miss
Pride*?'

Although she was too tense to have much appetite,
Joselin helped herself to scrambled egg from a bain-
marie on the sideboard, added a slice of toast and took
her place at the table. 'Why do you keep calling me
that?'

Sonia's mouth tautened, as if she would have
preferred to broach the subject in her own time. 'It's
still your name, isn't it?' she asked.

Now that the moment of confrontation had arrived,
Joselin felt strangely calm. 'What makes you think so?'

'I told you. The story was in the local paper.'
Reaching for her handbag, she pulled out a copy of the
newspaper and unfolded it on the table between them,
flicking over the pages until she reached the social
column. There was a photograph of the wedding party
at Pixie's bedside and the participants were named in a

caption underneath. They included 'marriage celebrant, Mr Anthony Briar'.

Her heart was thudding but Joselin arched an
eyebrow, pretending mild interest. 'So?'

'So how come your "marriage celebrant" is also
mentioned in the entertainment section—as a supporting actor in a new Australian feature film?'

'He could be a marriage celebrant as well as an
actor.'

'But we both know he isn't, don't we? Besides, I
checked and he isn't registered as one.' Sonia bit her
full lip pensively. 'I thought at first that this was
something you and Talan had cooked up between you
to fool Pixie. But Talan's the one being fooled. He
really thinks he's married to you, doesn't he?'

Defeated, Joselin lowered her head. She had been
hoping against hope that Sonia was bluffing, but it
was clear that she had pieced together the whole story
'What do you want?' she asked in a low voice.

Sonia's eyes flashed with triumph. 'I want you to go
back to Melbourne, back to your bit parts or whatever
it is you do. My relationship with Talan was
developing very nicely until you turned up and spoiled
everything.'

Joselin shot her a look of appeal which was totally
wasted on Sonia. 'But he told you that our marriage
was an arrangement of convenience.'

'Whose convenience, I wonder?' Sonia looked out
across the rolling paddocks, their chequerboard
colours visible through the window of the breakfast
room. 'I rather fancy myself as mistress of Yarrakina,
especially now that Talan's made the place a bit more
respectable. Of course, we'll have to find somewhere
for Pixie to live when she leaves the hospital, but it
shouldn't be hard to find a good nursing home for
her.'

How could anyone be so callous? 'You've got everything worked out, haven't you?' Joselin queried, revulsion in her tone.

Unperturbed, Sonia nodded. 'Of course. I usually do.'

'But why? You don't seem to love Talan, and you already have a property in Jilluka.'

Sonia's lip curled. 'I also have an older brother, darling. Geoffrey will inherit the property, as is his right. Oh, I won't be short of money, Daddy will see to that. But I must find a suitable place for myself, and I've decided that Yarrakina is ideal.'

The question tore at Joselin's heartstrings, but she had to ask it. 'And Talan . . . is he ideal too?'

'Naturally, I'm not as starry-eyed about him as you evidently are, but he *is* good looking and competent. We should be very well suited.'

Suitable was a word she seemed to apply often, Joselin noticed. She couldn't believe Sonia was talking about marriage in such a cold, calculating way that seemed to belong more to discussions about stocks and shares. Maybe that's how she saw marriage—as an investment in her future, with love coming second to security and future prospects. Inwardly, Joselin shuddered. 'What if I refuse to leave?'

'Then I'll tell Talan the whole story anyway, and you'll have no choice but to go. Either way, I win.'

So it seemed. 'Why didn't you tell him straight away?'

A look of distaste crossed Sonia's attractive features. 'I hate unpleasant scenes. This way is so much better, don't you think?'

Better for whom? she wondered, saying aloud, 'I don't seem to have much choice, do I?'

'Evidently. I'm so glad you're going to be sensible. Of course, you'll have to stay for a day or so more, until Pixie's well enough for you to leave her—I'm not as heartless as all that.' She patted her mouth delicately with her table napkin. 'Now that you and I understand each other, I'm sure I can rely on you not to take advantage of your position here?'

In other words, 'hands off Talan'. She understood Sonia's meaning only too well. Miserably, she nodded. 'Don't worry, I won't try to lure him to my bed or anything,' she said bitterly, thinking how ironic it was that only days ago, she'd been worried about how to prevent him from claiming what he thought was his right. Now that Sonia was offering her a way out, she felt cheated. She found she'd been enjoying these last couple of days as Talan's 'wife', fraud though she was.

As if they had been discussing the weather, Sonia said, 'Now we've got all that straightened out, I'm going for a ride. I've asked Bart to saddle two quiet horses for us—are you coming?'

Joselin felt the colour leave her face. She hadn't been on a horse since the accident and she wasn't sure whether she could bring herself to get on one ever again.

The sense of panic began to come back and she swallowed hard, trying to fight it down. 'I . . . I don't think so.'

Eyeing her curiously, Sonia said, 'Are you scared of horses or don't you ride at all? I should have thought you would, since you've spent so much time at Yarrakina on and off.'

'Yes I . . . I did. I used to ride a lot but I've . . . given it up.'

She could have said that it had given her up, along with all the other outdoor activities she had once found so challenging and enjoyable. Once her riding skills had got her many of her stunt jobs. She could just imagine Sonia's face if she showed her some of the hair-raising tricks she could do on horseback . . . used to be able to do, she added bitterly to herself.

Since Sonia was waiting for some sort of explanation, she said lamely, 'I had an accident not long ago. It affected my riding.' She didn't feel inclined to say in what way.

'You don't look impaired, but then Talan would hardly keep you around if you were,' Sonia tossed her mane of auburn hair. 'After all, he's as much a connoisseur of women as he is of merinos.'

Sonia couldn't know it, but her remark stabbed Joselin to the heart. She knew only too well that Talan despised weakness of any kind—he would be even less forgiving when the weakness was mental, instead of physical. Possessed of boundless courage himself, he would have no time for a woman who turned to jelly at the very thought of getting on a horse.

Scraping her chair back, Sonia stood up. 'It's a shame you won't come. I hate riding alone.'

Heedless of the dishes cluttering the table, she made for the door, obviously accustomed to having someone clear up after her at home. 'I'll see you when I get back.'

Joselin began to stack the dishes ready for Jean Spencer to do when she came in to tidy the house, then looked up as Sonia appeared in the doorway again. 'Yes?' she queried.

'I should have mentioned, there was a phone call for you earlier—a man called Garth Wizzard . . . or that's what it sounded like. He's coming out to see you, apparently something to do with insurance.'

Joselin's heart sank. 'Garth Vizzard,' she corrected automatically. 'He's here—in the area?'

'Stawell, I think he said, so it won't take him long to drive over. I gave him driving directions so he won't get lost.' She looked at Joselin keenly. 'What is he, some old flame come to fight Talan to get you back?'

If she hadn't been so appalled, Joselin would have laughed aloud at this idea. 'No, it isn't like that. I'm just not keen to see him, that's all.'

Sonia pouted. 'I suppose I did the wrong thing, telling him how to get here.'

'You weren't to know.' Stacking the last of the dishes, she reached a sudden decision. 'Is the offer to go riding with you still open?'

'But you said you didn't want to.'

'I've changed my mind.'

'All right, but what about your visitor?'

Joselin's resolve hardened. 'He's only a salesman who's been pestering me. He's probably on holiday in the area and decided to look me up. If I'm not here, he'll go away again and leave me alone.'

Sonia looked dubious, but nodded. 'If that's what you want. As I said, I hate to ride alone so any company is welcome.'

Even if it's mine, thought Joselin wickedly, then sobered. It was all very well to say she would go for a ride, but quite another thing to find the courage to get on the horse. 'I'll have to change first,' she said, in reality needing the time to marshal her reserves of courage.

'Okay, but don't be too long. I promised Talan that I'd join him at the muster camp for lunch.'

That decided her. Taking the stairs two at a time, Joselin went back to her room. She couldn't think why she had packed her riding clothes, since she hadn't expected to use them. Probably sheer force of habit had made her put them into the suitcase, she decided as she changed into them.

A few minutes later, she joined Sonia at the horse paddock where Bart Spencer had saddled two quiet horses for them—a roan for Sonia and a beautiful grey called Quicksilver for Joselin. Even as she admired the horse's sleek lines, she felt her heart begin to race. Her hands felt clammy and slipped on the reins Bart handed to her.

She spent a few minutes patting the horse's velvet nose, to steady herself, all the while whispering to herself, 'I can do it. I can do it.' At the same time, the traitorous inner voice which had haunted her since the accident was whispering, 'No, you can't. You're terrified. Run away. Hide.'

'No, I won't!' she said aloud, startling the horse and attracting Sonia's attention. She was already mounted and waiting impatiently for Joselin to join her.

'What was that?'

'I ... I was talking to the horse. I'm coming,' Joselin said through parched lips. There was nothing for it. Having said she would come, she had to get on to the horse. It was either that, or stay here and face Garth Vizzard when he turned up.

The thought of Garth acted as a catalyst. Deliberately, she made her mind a blank and moved around to the side of the horse, not giving herself time to think as she swung herself into the saddle. Then habit took over and she urged Quicksilver forward to join Sonia. 'I'm doing it. I'm actually riding!' she told herself in astonishment. Her heart was still beating much too fast and her palms were wet, but she hadn't turned and run—she was riding the horse, even if it wasn't with her old insouciance. She was aboard and that was all that mattered for now.

'You look very pleased with yourself,' Sonia said as Joselin's horse kept pace with hers.

'Why not? It's such a lovely morning,' she said cheerfully. Right now, she felt as if she could conquer the whole world. Maybe she could even find a way to make peace with Talan before Sonia presented her damning evidence.

She had to remind herself not to get carried away by this small triumph over her own fears. Although sorely tempted to let Quicksilver have his head and gallop wildly over the paddock as she used to do, she kept a tight rein on the horse. Better take things slowly until she was sure this new-found confidence was going to last.

At the same time, she had a strong feeling that it would. Maybe by getting on to the horse in defiance of her terror, she had taken the first painful step along the road to recovery.

Dared she hope that she might eventually conquer *all* of her fears and become whole again? She would be worthy of a man like Talan then, and not even Sonia's blackmail would stand in her way.

It was too early to be thinking like that. She had a long way to go before she was ready to take on a woman as self-assured as Sonia. 'Easy . . .' she said aloud, as if talking to the horse. Only she knew that the caution was meant for herself.

CHAPTER SIX

THE ringing call of the currawongs and the raucous laugh of the kookaburras were the only sounds which disturbed the air for a while as they rode. After a few miles, during which she realised that the sure-footed horse could manage perfectly well without her constant attention, Joselin forced herself to relax. Gradually, her vice-like grip on the reins eased, and she began to enjoy the ride, although she was on the alert for the sense of panic to return.

It seemed unbelievable that she could actually be riding again, if not with her old assurance, at least without the terror she'd experienced on mounting.

Sonia slowed so that Joselin came abreast of her, 'I thought you said you weren't much of a rider.'

'I said I'd given it up. I suppose it's like riding a bicycle—once learned, never forgotten.'

Sonia snorted in disbelief. 'Look, Joselin Pride, I've been a judge at out local shows and I know a good rider when I see one. I'd say you're a lot better than good, although you're on tenterhooks for some reason. Have you ever ridden professionally?'

Joselin lowered her head. 'How do you mean?'

'I mean in shows, things like that.'

Relief washed over Joselin. 'No, I've never ridden in a show in my life.' It was no lie. She'd ridden professionally as a stunt woman, of course, but never in shows.

'Still, I get the feeling there's more to you than meets the eye,' Sonia observed. When Joselin gave this line of discussion no encouragement, she kicked her

horse's flanks and rode on, leaving Joselin to follow
behind.

Why was Sonia so interested in her background? she
wondered uneasily. Since she'd already made her
position at Yarrakina quite clear, surely she didn't
regard Joselin as competition any longer? Sighing,
Joselin dismissed the whole question from her mind
and let her gaze wander idly over the magnificent
scenery.

The Grampians were a world unto themselves, she
thought as she had many times. It was said that sheep
raised in the shadow of these ranges provided the
finest wool in the world. Remembering the weighty
fleeces she'd watched the wool classers handling
during shearing, she could believe it. Every fibre was
inches long and incredibly thick. She'd been told that
one fleece could weigh ten pounds or more. She would
like to be here at shearing time. Already the musters
were underway to bring the animals in to the holding
yards where they would be stripped of their fleeces
and returned, thin and goatish, to the paddocks.

The shearers were always interesting characters.
Soon they would arrive, singly or in teams, having
worked their way down the tablelands starting with
Queensland for the January clip, and ending up in
Victoria for the spring shearing. She remembered only
too well the controlled chaos that would follow; the
unbelievable noise of shouting men, bleating sheep
and roaring machinery. Then, the station would be
crowded and bustling, the shed paddocks brimming
with sheep. It would be good to be a part of it all
again. At the same time, she realised that she never
would be. She was no longer a schoolgirl, entitled to
spend her holidays here. The property belonged to
Talan Devereaux now, and if Sonia had her way, she
would rule it at his side.

The thought stung her like the bite of a March fly and she flinched visibly. Why was it so painful to think of Sonia and Talan as a pair? She'd forfeited her right to share in his life when she decided to deceive him—first over her background, and then with the fake marriage. Now she was paying the price.

But that was before she had admitted to herself that she loved him. Would it have made any difference? No, she conceded to herself. It would have been much worse if she had really married him, then discovered that he despised her because of what she had become.

'Hurry up, slow coach!' called Sonia and, startled, Joselin looked up to find that the gap between their horses had lengthened considerably. She urged Quicksilver forward to reduce the distance. Soon they topped a rise—they were almost at the muster camp, so-called, although it was really no more than a temporary arrangement of holding yards and make-shift amenities for the men. The noise and dust were overwhelming, as the closely mustered sheep bleated and milled around. They were kept in check by the well-trained kelpie dogs who moved noiselessly around the fringes of the mob, nipping at the heels of any sheep which dared to stray.

For a moment, Joselin felt the sense of panic returning. She hadn't counted on being caught in the middle of all this. A motor bike roared nearby, causing her horse to shy and she had to keep it tightly reined in. Her heart began to thud painfully and her wet palms slipped on the reins. She fought down the urge to pull the horse's head around and gallop for the safety of the homestead.

Then she saw him. Unlike most of his men, Talan was working on horseback, evidently preferring the old-fashioned style of doing things. He looked splendid in the saddle of his black mare, man and animal working together as if they were one. Beneath the wide brim of his hat, his dust-streaked face looked as if it was sculpted from bronze.

Her heart leapt at the sight of him. She couldn't turn and run while he was here.

Spotting her, he rode up to her. 'Sonia told me she'd join us for a smoko, but I didn't expect to see you here. You haven't shown any interest in riding since you got here.'

'There hasn't been all that much time,' she reminded him, unaccountably hurt that he wasn't more welcoming. It almost sounded as if he would have preferred Sonia to turn up alone.

'True enough. Well since you're here, you may as well join us for some lunch. Hungry?'

She nodded, although she didn't have much appetite. That soon changed when she dismounted, dropping Quicksilver's reins over his head, and leaving him to graze in the shade of some river red gums. The smell of sausages sizzling in a pan was tantalising and she sniffed appreciatively.

It was simple fare but tasted delicious in the sharp, eucalyptus-scented air. Thick pork sausages wrapped in wedges of fresh wholemeal bread and smothered with tomato sauce was the order of the day. She accepted a plateful, and a mug of 'billy' tea, and settled in the shade of a tree to eat her lunch.

Sonia sat down close to Talan, she noted with a pang, wishing she'd had the courage to join him herself. He probably wouldn't have welcomed her company anyway after sounding put out that she'd come along at all. Bart Spencer dropped down on the grass beside her, his plate heaped with bread and sausages. 'Enjoying yourself?'

'To be frank, not very,' she said, glad to have someone she could be honest with at last.

He nodded, misunderstanding her reason. 'Not much of a place for a woman, this. You wouldn't catch Lillian or young Jean out here in a fit.'

She decided not to correct him. 'All the same, I should be used to the heat and dust. Old "Doc" Frencham used to take me out with him often when I came here for my school holidays.'

Bart's weathered face lit up at her use of the name. 'There's a fine bloke, all right,' he marvelled. 'D'you know how he came by the name of Doc?'

'No, he never did tell me.'

'It was on a muster the likes of this one. One of his young jackeroos had an argument with a boning knife when he was supposed to be cutting up a carcass for a barbecue. Near sliced his leg off, he did.'

She guessed what was coming. 'And "Doc" fixed him up?'

'You bet. Calm as you like. He stitched the leg up and carried the lad back to the homestead on his own horse. They called the real doctor, but he reckoned he couldn't have done a better job of stitching the wound himself, so he didn't even touch it.'

Joselin's eyes widened. 'And did the boy's leg heal all right?'

Grinning broadly, Bart nodded. 'Reckon it did. You're looking at him.' He hitched up his moleskin trouser leg to reveal a long-healed scar two thirds the way around one calf. 'Pity old Doc wouldn't stay around when Mr Devereaux became boss.'

'Didn't they get along?' she asked curiously.

'Wasn't that. Doc reckoned he couldn't work for anybody but Missus Pride—so he wouldn't work for anybody, period. He's retired now, living at Halls Gap and growing vegetables.'

'But you don't mind working for Talan?' she couldn't resist asking.

'He's a fair bloke. Won't ask his men to do anything he wouldn't do. I worked for his old man before the fires burnt them out, so when I found out Doc wasn't staying on, I applied for the job. Lil and the girls do a bit of work at the homestead, so it's worked out very nicely.'

He eased his hat back from his forehead and swatted at the ever-present flies which divebombed his face. 'That explains what I'm doing here, but what about you? Pardon my saying so, but you and the boss don't seem all that happy for a pair of newlyweds.'

She averted her face. 'We're not. I think I made a mistake even coming back here.'

'Maybe you should give it some time. Like I said, the boss is nothing if not fair. He never dismisses a bloke—even an incompetent one—without a fair trial. Reckon he'd do at least the same for a wife.'

Wiping the last of the tomato sauce off his plate with a hunk of bread, he popped it into his mouth and stood up, touching his hand to his hat in salute. Then he returned to the other men.

For several minutes, she sat where she was, mulling over his advice. He'd known Talan since he was a boy, so he was well able to advise her. Maybe she should take it seriously. If Talan was as fair and just as Bart seemed to think, maybe she should give him the chance to judge her. She assumed that he would despise her for what she'd become. Maybe he would be kinder than that. At least it would be better than having him hear the truth from Sonia, whose version was bound to be tinged with venom.

Eagerly, she jumped to her feet and returned her plate to the roustabout who was now washing the dishes. He waved away her offer of help and she realised she'd only made it to put off approaching Talan.

It might be the wrong time, of course, but she knew perfectly well that if she waited another minute, her courage would desert her. Resolutely, she walked over to where he stood, looking out towards the ranges, one hand massaging the back of his neck to ease his muscles.

Coming up behind him, she began to knead his shoulders with sure fingers, having done the same for aching stuntmen on many a set. At first, he tensed at her touch then, gradually, he began to relax and she felt the muscles smoothing out under her hands. She had to stand on tiptoe to reach his shoulders and her calves protested after a while but she ignored them and kept up the massaging movements.

After a few minutes, he turned around and suddenly she was in his arms. 'You have very good hands,' he said huskily, his eyes dark and unreadable.

She looked quickly over her shoulder. They were screened from the others by a line of wattle trees and the horses grazed between them and the rest of the camp. 'I had to talk to you,' she said, her eyes wide with appeal. 'Maybe this isn't the time or the place . . .'

He seemed to sense that her defences were down and he tightened his hold on her shoulders. 'If it helps to straighten things out between us, then it's the right time. You don't know how I've longed for you to look at me like this—with honest caring in your eyes, instead of the invisible barriers you've been putting up between us.'

She looked up at him through thickly fringed lashes. 'It hasn't been easy, keeping you at arm's length,' she admitted. 'When what I really wanted was . . .'

'Was what?' he asked thickly.

'You in my bed.' There, she'd said it. Let him think she was shameless if he chose.

Her admission caught him by surprise. 'I never guessed. I thought I was the only one who cared.'

She began to make her confession but he put a finger to her lips. 'Don't say any more just yet. I want to savour that last bit for a moment.' His face twisted with frustration. 'God, if only we weren't in the middle of all these people! But there is one thing I *can* do here and now.'

'Talan, wait. There's something I must tell you.' But she was wasting her breath, and she was left with precious little to waste because he covered her mouth with his, silencing her protests. They were both dusty and sweaty, but neither of them noticed as their breath mingled. His lips were warm and demanding, and she found her own lips parting in instinctive response. At once, his tongue invaded her mouth, at first gently probing, then twining around hers in a love dance which sent eddies of desire whirling through her.

She swayed slightly under the onslaught of his kiss, and his grip on her shoulders tightened, his fingers digging deep into her tender flesh. He could have gone through to the bone for all she cared. She was only conscious of a hunger for him which drove every other thought from her head.

Their bodies merged into one line, making her achingly aware of the effect she was having on him. Her hips ground against his until he groaned aloud with frustration. He lifted his head and she was warmed by the naked desire in his eyes. 'We've got to get away from here,' he urged.

'Oh, there you are!' said an over-bright voice. Guiltily, Joselin sprang away from Talan but her flushed face and shining eyes would have given her away, even if Sonia hadn't seen them locked together a moment before.

Talan raked a hand through his hair, his annoyance

plain. 'What do you want, Sonia?'

'I want to talk to you,' she said, her eyes fixed on Joselin and blazing with hatred. 'There's something you should know about your sweet little girlfriend here.'

She couldn't stand here and watch the love in his eyes turn to disgust, she couldn't. She turned quickly.

'Joselin, wait!'

At his heartfelt cry, she almost turned back, then urged herself to keep going. After what she had witnessed, Sonia would show her no mercy. There was no point in staying around for the *coup de grâce*.

The bleats of the sheep, the shouts of the men and the whinnying horses merged into one confusing sound as she ran for her horse, still placidly cropping the dry grass. In one motion, she tossed the reins over the animal's head and threw her leg across the saddle, urging Quicksilver to a trot almost before she was fully mounted.

Leaving the muster camp behind, she pointed Quicksilver's head towards home and then let him follow his instincts. She was too blinded by tears to see where she was going anyway. Then she fancied she heard the sound of hoofbeats behind her and she urged the horse to a gallop, lying along its neck with the ease of long familiarity.

The ground flew beneath her horse's hooves and her ears were filled with the thunderous beat. The landscape blurred around her and soon there was nothing but the two of them, streaming along, crushing the wildflowers beneath them so they sent up pungent scents which were quickly left behind them.

After what seemed like an age, she reined the horse in. She had been riding flat out for what seemed like miles and fearfully, she glanced backwards but there was no one in pursuit. She had outrun them.

She slowed the horse to a walk while she savoured

this last thought. She had outrun them. She, who this morning had been too scared to mount the horse, had covered miles of rough terrain at full gallop, her thoughts too concentrated on Talan to spare any for herself.

Despite her inner turmoil, a smile spread across her even features. She was cured! Somehow, Talan's love had helped her to conquer her fears so she could be whole again. Worrying about him, she'd had no time to worry about herself and in consequence, had performed feats she had thought were beyond her forever.

Her pleasure was short-lived, however. Right now, Sonia was probably telling Talan the whole story. She could imagine his handsome features, so recently alight with desire for her, turning dark and angry as he aborbed what Sonia was saying. He, who hated to be manipulated by a woman, would think her the worst of the lot. Sonia didn't know about the accident, so she couldn't tell him what a spineless creature Joselin was ... had been until now, she amended. But the fake wedding would be enough to destroy his love for her.

Fate was unbelievably cruel, she thought bitterly. In one stroke, it had restored her courage and taken away the only reason she wanted to be strong and whole. What was she to do now?

In despair, she spurred Quicksilver to a gallop again and gave herself up to the ride without thinking any more about Talan. That way lay madness. For now, she could savour the feeling of being once more in control of herself, flying free and unafraid over the landscape.

As she experimented with riding one-handed, and then with the reins between her knees, she began to wish for a stunt-trained horse so she could try one or two falls at full gallop. They had been something of a speciality of hers before. She felt sure she could do them again now.

She contented herself with clinging to Quicksilver's flank with her body only inches from the hard ground. When she sensed the horse becoming nervous, she swung herself upright in the saddle again. That last trick had been a favourite with film producers. If filmed from the opposite side, the horse appeared to be riderless. It was also an old Indian trick which enabled the rider to sneak up on his victim, she recalled the stunt's origin.

Playing games in the saddle was one thing. Facing reality was another, she told herself. It was all very well to be cured of her fears, but it wasn't going to help her relationship with Talan once Sonia got through with her tale-telling.

She slowed the horse to a walk, and turned his head for home. The sooner she faced Talan's wrath, the sooner she could pack and return to Melbourne. There was no way he'd want her around after today.

By the time she got back, the sun was low over the homestead, tipping the eucalyptus trees with golden fire and spilling orange light over the rooftops of the main house and outbuildings. Even the silo looked softer and more at home in its surroundings in the pale evening light.

Joselin was in no mood to appreciate the beauty of the scene. With every step, she came closer to the showdown she'd been dreading. By now, Talan must know how she'd deceived him—Sonia would have seen to that. Would he give her a chance to explain why she felt she had to do it?

As she crested the last rise before the homestead, she noticed a strange vehicle parked in front of the house. It could have belonged to someone visiting the Spencers, or even calling on Talan, but somehow, she knew with a dreadful certainty, that the insurance agent she'd been avoiding was still at the house.

She debated whether to stay away a little longer in the hope that he would tire of waiting and leave. But he'd obviously been there most of the day so he wasn't likely to leave until he'd seen her, however late that was.

Her stomach churned at the thought, even though she had nothing really to fear from him. It was more that he reminded her of so much she needed to forget. This, more than anything else, was the reason she'd been avoiding him all day.

Suddenly, all thoughts of the insurance agent were driven from her mind by the sight of Talan striding across the clearing to his utility, parked under a tree. As she watched, he threw a case into the back of it and got into the driver's seat. A moment later, he drove off in a flurry of dust.

A lump rose to her throat and threatened to choke her. So that was that. He was so angry with her that he was leaving before she got home, rather than face her. Desperation made her urge Quicksilver forward into a gallop. She had to catch him before he left. She had to. A fence loomed ahead and without taking time to think, she put the horse to it. Horse and rider sailed over effortlessly but she gave herself no time to savour this new triumph. She was only interested in catching up with Talan so she could explain herself to him.

But he was already picking up speed as she neared the homestead, and she reined the horse in. If Talan was so anxious to avoid her, she would only demean herself further in his eyes by racing after him.

Sonia came out to greet her as she rode slowly up to the house. The woman's smug expression told Joselin more clearly than words that she was pleased with her day's work.

'Had a good ride?' she called cheerfully, as Bart Spencer came to take the reins from Joselin and lead Quicksilver away.

She couldn't even pretend politeness. 'What do you think? I saw Talan driving away just now. He seemed to be in a hurry.'

'Wouldn't you be keen to get away if your wife's boyfriend had just turned up?'

Joselin stared at her, uncomprehendingly. 'What do you mean?'

'I mean, when he found out that this agent-fellow, Garth Vizzard, is an old flame of yours, he took off like a wounded bull.'

'But I told you the man means nothing to me. I don't even want to see him.'

'But he wants to see you. He knows an awful lot about your private life for a mere business acquaintance and he was only too happy to show off his knowledge to Talan. Coming on top of what he found out about you today, I'd say it was the last straw.'

Too shaken even to speak. Joselin stared at Sonia in horror. Everything the agent knew about her came from snooping into her affairs, but Talan wasn't to know that. He must think they were on intimate terms for the man to know so much about her.

Distractedly, she ran a hand through her hair. 'Did he say when he would be back?'

Sonia's satisfied smile widened. 'I don't think he will, at least not tonight. I think he's hoping you'll be gone by the time he gets back here tomorrow.'

You'd like that, wouldn't you? Joselin thought but saying it aloud wouldn't help. 'I may not be going just yet,' she said instead and had the small satisfaction of seeing Sonia's face fall. 'I think I owe Talan an explanation, at least.'

'Don't be surprised if he doesn't want to hear it,' Sonia snapped and turned on her heel.

Wearily, Joselin followed Sonia into the house, knowing she couldn't put off a meeting with the agent for much longer. After so much inactivity, the day's ride had tired her more than she expected. She was so accustomed to breezing through all kinds of hard physical activity that it came as a shock to feel her muscles protesting.

She looked longingly at the staircase, thinking how good a hot bath would feel right now, then resignedly turned towards the living room.

Garth Vizzard was standing with his back to her, looking out of the big picture windows. He turned as she came in and she noticed that he had a camera slung around his neck, its barrel nose suggesting it was fitted with a telephoto lens.

'Hello there, Miss Pride,' the man said, holding out his hand in greeting.

She ignored the outstretched hand. 'Good day, Mr Vizzard. Would you mind telling me just what you're doing here?'

'My job, girlie, my job, as I've told you before.'

'But what on earth did you expect to find here?'

He tapped the camera significantly. 'I found it. You made a splendid picture, sailing over that fence on your horse. It was just what I needed.'

Her brow wrinkled expressively. 'I don't understand.'

'I'll bet you don't. In the city, you were so pathetic and helpless, careful never to let anyone catch you doing anything the least bit strenuous. Out here, you probably thought you were safe enough, so you've been riding the range doing your daredevil stunts without a care in the world. You didn't expect me to turn up here, did you? My picture will give the lie to any claim you make from here on about not being fit to work any more.'

'But I told you, I wasn't going to make any claims on your company. I . . . I really couldn't work any more after the accident. That wasn't a lie.' She chose her words carefully. 'Something happened here which helped me get back to normal.'

He was unperturbed. 'Well, this picture of mine will ensure you get back to normal even quicker. If you try suing our client for loss of earning power or the like, we'll produce this photo in court as evidence that you're faking.'

What was the use! The man had a one-track mind. 'If you say so,' she said, defeated. 'Now that you have your "evidence", does it mean you're going to leave me alone?'

'As long as you leave us alone, girlie,' he confirmed.

Only as she let out a long sigh of relief did she realise she'd been holding her breath. 'I'm glad some good is going to come of all this.' Not enough to salvage her relationship with Talan, but at least she would no longer be haunted by this horrible man.

They looked up as Sonia breezed into the room, carrying a small overnight bag. 'Excuse me,' she said brightly, smiling from one to the other. 'I know you two have a lot to talk about so I'm taking myself off.'

'But we don't . . .' began Joselin, knowing it was useless.

'I know you don't mind me being here,' continued Sonia smoothly, 'but I hate playing gooseberry. Talan went ahead as he had things to do in town, but now I'd better follow him. We have plans for the evening,' she finished significantly.

Joselin bit her lip, feeling a trickle of blood bead the inside of her lip. But the pain was nothing compared to the agony in her heart at the thought of Talan and

Sonia spending the evening together and probably the night as well.

'There's no need to rush away on my account,' Garth Vizzard assured Sonia.

'Nonsense. I live with my father and brother so I know what it's like always having a third party around to cramp your style.'

Why was Sonia so determined to pair them off when she knew perfectly well that there was nothing between Joselin and the insurance agent? Maybe it was an attempt to ease her conscience for coming between Joselin and Talan. Well, it wasn't going to work. 'There's no need for you to worry about Mr Vizzard,' she said carefully. 'He's just leaving now anyway, aren't you?' She shot him an icy look.

He shrugged cheerfully. 'As you wish, girlie. I've got what I came for anyway.'

Sonia speedily adjusted to the changed situation. 'In that case, maybe you'd give me a lift into town. If you're going that way?' She batted her eyelashes coquettishly, making Joselin feel slightly ill.

The agent regarded Sonia with interest. 'It would be a pleasure.'

He took the overnight case from Sonia and opened the door for her, showing more courtesy in the last few minutes than he'd demonstrated in all the months he'd been shadowing Joselin.

She watched them leave from her vantage point at the living-room window. She was glad Sonia hadn't succeeded in leaving them alone. Heaven knew what lengths the man was prepared to go to to collect his precious evidence.

Not that he would ever have cause to use it. Even if she could have gained millions of dollars from suing his company, it couldn't have compensated for the hell she'd been through since the accident.

There was no way she could stand up in court and describe her feelings publicly. It would have been too humiliating. She would rather have died than relive the accident over and over again in a courtroom. Maybe if her injuries had been physical, it would have been different. At least they would have healed in time, allowing her to resume her career.

But they *had* healed, she reminded herself, thinking of her wild ride over the paddocks this afternoon. Miraculously, she had regained the courage which had made her one of the country's top stunt women. The certainty flowed through her like a charge of adrenalin. Once she got back into training, she would be as good as before, she felt sure.

If only she could heal things between herself and Talan. But their relationship wasn't a scene in a film, to be improved by a director calling for a retake. If it had been, she would have done a great many things differently, including being honest with him from the beginning.

CHAPTER SEVEN

JOSELIN knew that the men were watching her practise but it give her little pleasure. If Talan had been among them, it would have been a different matter. But he wasn't among the group of stockmen gathered around the horse paddock, so she went through her warm-up routine mechanically, concentrating on each movement to the exclusion of everything else.

Even twenty-four hours ago, she would have revelled in using her body like this. She'd given up most of her exercise routines when they seemed to have no purpose any more. Now she knew it was only a matter of time before she returned to work again, so the exercises were essential to get her back into top shape. But since Talen had driven away, there was no joy in any of it for her.

Dressed in a black skivvy and black stretch pants, with sandshoes on her feet, she vaulted up on to the top rail of the horse paddock, her effortless grace earning her a burst of applause from the men. Soon, they fell silent, their silence even more of a tribute than their applause, as she somersaulted over and over on the wooden railing. Then she executed a smooth back flip and landed on her feet in the dust.

'You're as good as that champion, Nadia Something,' Bart said admiringly.

Joselin swabbed the back of her neck with a towel. 'Thanks, but I'm hardly Olympic class.'

The head stockman's eyes were wide with admiration. 'All the same, you'll do me.'

Smiling her thanks, she headed back to the

homestead to shower and change. Behind her, she heard the men dispersing to their various duties.

Yarrakina ran almost as well whether Talan was there or not, she thought, then recognised the thought as unfair. It was his careful choice of men and skilled handling of them which ensured they worked as well without supervision as when he was there watching them.

What was he doing now? she wondered as she stood under the gushing shower. She'd sat up late last night, hoping that he would come back so they could talk. But of course he hadn't. He was much too busy with whatever plans Sonia had been referring to when she went to join him. The thought of them together was acutely painful, and she twisted the shower off with a savage gesture, then returned to her room to get dressed.

She had already decided what she would do. The men had returned her car to the homestead—someone had even repaired the scratches to the paintwork. So there was nothing to stop her from driving into Stawell to make sure that Pixie was all right, then driving straight back to Melbourne.

Half an hour later, she was dressed in her red tartan pants and a white turtle-necked sweater, with the rest of her clothes packed into her suitcase.

Lillian came out of the kitchen as Joselin descended the staircase. 'Will you be staying in town with Mr Devereaux then?' she asked, catching sight of the suitcase.

'I . . . I'm not really sure,' she muttered, trying to avoid an outright lie but not wanting to discourage the housekeeper's assumption that she and her 'husband' would be together. Everyone would know the truth soon anyway, but she would leave it to Talan to explain things.

Lillian smiled. 'I see. It all depends on Mrs Pride, I expect.'

'Something like that.'

'In that case, I won't prepare anything for dinner tonight. I'll leave some cold food in the fridge just in case, though. Will that be all right?'

'Oh yes, fine.'

Lillian wiped floury hands on her apron. 'Actually, it will work out very well. I was hoping to be able to get away for a few days as it happens.'

Anxious to be off, Joselin tried to curb her impatience. 'I'm sure there won't be any problem. Are you going by yourself?'

'Goodness, no. The last time I was away by myself was when I was in hospital having Jean. No, she and Bart are coming with me. It's our niece's wedding, you see.'

Joselin's brow wrinkled. 'Does Talan ... Mr Devereaux know you'll all be away?'

'Of course. Now that the lamb marking's in hand, it's the only chance we'll have till after the shearing.'

'I see.' The truth was, she didn't really. Surely Talan couldn't plan to be away for very long if he'd given his head stockman some time off? There were other senior people working at Yarrakina, of course, but Bart was Talan's most experienced and valued man.

But it wasn't up to her to interfere. Talan must know what he was doing. 'Have a good time, won't you,' she said brightly, picking up her case.

Lillian waved her away, then went back inside, presumably to prepare a store of cold foods to tide Talan over while she was away.

The drive back to Stawell seemed much longer now she was on her own, without Talan beside her. She had better get used to it, she supposed, since he had evidently gone out of her life for good as soon as he had heard about her treachery.

If only she could have explained to him why she did it! Sonia would have told it in a way which made Joselin look like a scheming female, gloating over the way she'd outwitted him. He would never believe that her behaviour was no more than self-defence, to save herself from getting hurt. Her breath hissed out between her teeth in a despairing sigh. What was the use? She would never have the chance to set the record straight so there was no point even thinking about it.

For the rest of the journey, she made her mind a deliberate blank and was relieved when the outskirts of the town came in sight. She easily remembered the way to the hospital and was soon parked outside the red brick building. Only as she approached it, did it occur to her that Talan might be visiting Pixie as well and her heart began to race at the prospect, but she steeled herself to go inside and take her chances.

But Pixie was alone when Joselin went into her room bearing an armload of flowers she'd bought on the way. She set them down on the bedside table. 'Hello, darling, how are you?'

Pixie's lined face broke into a smile. 'All the better for seeing you, my dear. Talen said you'd probably come along later.'

Joselin's heart did somersaults in her chest, but she schooled her features into a cheerful mask. 'What time was he here?'

'Not long ago. He came as soon as he finished his business in town. But I suppose you know all about that.'

Since she didn't have a clue what he was doing in town, she couldn't very well agree, but she made a non-committal noise and began to fuss with the flowers, removing some wilted ones from the vase and replacing them with her fresh blooms. 'I do hope you like these,' she said, keeping her back to Pixie.

'You know I love all flowers,' Pixie said warmly. 'Of course I'd much rather enjoy them growing wild, then cut to put in vases.'

'You'll be back among your wild flowers soon enough,' Joselin reminded her.

'Sonia didn't seem to think so when she was here—although she did bring me this lovely pot plant.'

If her aunt had thrust a knife into her ribs, the pain couldn't have been more intense. 'That was nice of her,' she said in a tight little voice.

'Yes, it was. Personally, I've never cared for the woman, although her father is a charming man—quite unaffected, despite the fact that he's wealthy. But Sonia's another matter. Talan told me she's staying at Yarrakina for a few days.'

So they'd been to see Pixie together. Joselin should have expected it, but she felt miserable at having it confirmed. 'Yes, she is. They're having a new wing added to their house and she didn't want to be around while the work was going on.'

Pixie snorted aloud. 'Typical. Never could stand a bit of dust or mess. She had some crazy idea of marrying Talan, but I think she's more in love with Yarrakina than with him as a man.'

'She did grow up on a station, so she's used to the life,' Joselin said unwillingly.

'In between boarding schools, you mean? Her idea of a man on the land is a Collins Street farmer.'

Joselin smiled at Pixie's reference to the wealthy businessmen who invested in farming from a distance. 'Still, she's more at home on the land than I'll ever be,' she said sorrowfully.

'Nonsense! Knowing the land and loving it are two different things. You love Yarrakina—don't you think Talan knew it when he married you?'

Except that they weren't married, and Talan knew it

now, which must be why he'd brought Sonia with him to see Pixie. Perhaps he was trying to get Pixie to accept them as a pair. 'That's enough about us,' she said firmly. 'Let's talk about you. Is the doctor happy with your progress?'

'Doctors are never happy with one's progress,' Pixie laughed. 'Hastings won't be happy until I agree to take things easy and stop gadding about in the ranges, to use his expression.'

While she could understand the doctor's reasoning, Joselin knew that nothing would stop her aunt wandering her beloved hills while she still had the breath to do so. 'He's only doing his job,' she said mildly. 'When does he say you can come home?'

She surprised a mistiness in her aunt's eyes, which was quickly banished. 'Depends what you mean by home. Sonia seemed to think I should plan to go into some sort of rest home when I leave here, so I can be near to medical help if I need it.'

Remembering Sonia's avowed intention to find a nursing home for Pixie, Joselin was hurt but unsurprised. It seemed the other woman was already putting her plans into effect. If only she could reassure her aunt that there would always be a place for her at Yarrakina, even though the property now belonged to Talan. But she was no longer in any position to make such a promise.

'We'll talk about that later,' she said, squeezing her aunt's hand tightly. 'You haven't asked me what I thought of your new discovery yet.'

At once, some of the sadness left Pixie's face, although her eyes were still haunted. 'Ah, my "cave of hands". Isn't it magnificent?'

'One of the finest and most intact examples I've ever seen,' Joselin assured her. 'Thank you for letting Talan show it to me.'

'Everyone will have to know about it sooner or later, but I wanted it to be special between us just for a while,' Pixie said.

'I understand. I . . . I have to go now. The doctor told me not to tire you out.'

'Seeing you gives me a new lease of life, more likely. Will you be back tomorrow?'

Joselin hesitated. 'I . . . of course,' she said decisively. She could always get a room in Stawell until her aunt was well enough not to depend on her visits.

On her way back to the car, she was stopped by a figure she recognised as Dr Hastings. 'May I talk to you for a moment, Mrs Devereaux?' he asked.

She raised a quizzical eyebrow. 'Of course. What's the trouble?'

'There's no trouble—yet,' the doctor said. 'I don't know how much you understand about medicine, but I'm sure you've heard of the will to live?' She nodded and he went on, 'I'm concerned that Pixie may be losing hers. Some of the fight has gone out of her lately, and while we're doing everything we can medically to make her well, she must contribute the wish to get better.'

'Why wouldn't she want to get better?'

'I think she's afraid that she won't be wanted anywhere after she leaves here. Money isn't a problem,' he said smoothly when Joselin tried to interrupt. 'I know she has enough to live on from the sale of Yarrakina. But a woman like Pixie thrives on being needed.'

Damn Sonia and her talk about nursing homes! 'What can I do?' she asked helplessly.

'Reassure her that she'll be welcome with you and your husband when she's discharged.' He looked at her keenly. 'You do want her with you, don't you?'

'Of course I do,' she said fiercely. 'It's just . . .'

'You still haven't resolved things between yourself and your husband,' he contributed. 'Well, all I can say is that, for Pixie's sake, I hope you can sort it out before she's ready to leave here. If you put her into a nursing home, you may as well kill her and be done with it.'

Before she could say a word, he turned on his heel and strode quickly away, leaving her dumbfounded. He hadn't even given her a chance to explain that her supposed husband had already left her. Sonia didn't want Pixie under her roof—so what could Joselin do? She would gladly invite Pixie to live with her in Melbourne, but her aunt would be miserable away from her beloved Grampians.

There was only one solution. She would have to swallow her pride and return to Yarrakina. Talan must come back sometime, and when he did she would find a way to make him listen to her. Maybe there was no hope for the two of them, but surely he would make Sonia understand why Pixie must go on living at Yarrakina?

It seemed strange to be driving back along the eucalyptus-lined driveway to the homestead, only hours after she thought she had left it behind forever.

Knowing that Bart, Lillian and their daughter, Jean, must have gone by now to attend their family wedding, she expected to find the homestead deserted so she was surprised to see a green station waggon parked outside.

Warily, she walked up to it, then relaxed when she recognised the driver. 'Tony! What on earth are you doing here?'

Tony Briar stepped out and handed her an enormous armful of flowers. 'I came to see you, of course. There was nobody around so I resigned myself to waiting in the car until somebody showed up—

and here you are.'

'And here you are,' she echoed, sniffing the flowers appreciatively. 'What brings you to the Grampians?'

'I was on location some miles south of here and we wrapped earlier than expected, so I thought I'd drop in on you before I headed back to Melbourne.' He coloured suddenly and ducked his head in an uncharacteristic gesture of shyness. 'You see, I have some news for you and I didn't want you to hear it on the grapevine.'

'You and Julie are getting married,' she said, a smile twitching up the corners of her mouth.

'Yes, but how did you know? I only proposed to her yesterday.'

'Women's intuition. That and the fact that you've had eyes for no one else ever since I introduced you to my gorgeous flatmate.' She linked her arm with his. 'Come inside and tell me all about it.'

While she brewed coffee, he sat at the kitchen table with his chin braced on both hands. 'I know marriage isn't exactly fashionable in our business, but at least Julie's in a different profession so there may be some hope for us. I love Julie and I think she cares for me.'

'You know she does, so stop fishing,' Joselin said with mock severity. 'All I get is Tony Briar this, and Tony Briar that from morning till night. It will be a relief when you two finally get married.'

As she set the steaming cups in front of them and pushed a plate of biscuits towards him, he arched an eyebrow at her. 'Speaking of marriages, how is yours working out? I think I did rather a good job of the ceremony, by the way.'

She sobered at once. 'Yes, you did, but not good enough, I'm afraid.'

'He found out and didn't appreciate the joke,' Tony guessed.

'Something like that.'

He took a sip of his coffee. 'What I don't understand is why you had to pretend in the first place. I got the impression that the guy was willing to marry you for real.'

'I know and I was a fool not to see it. I suppose I was scared that he'd regret it afterwards.'

'So you got in first, hurting him before he had a chance to hurt you. So what happens now?'

She looked down at her splayed hands. 'I wish I knew. Now Talan knows how I deceived him, he doesn't want me around any more and I can't really blame him for that. So I suppose I'll go back to Melbourne and get on with my life. Work is supposed to be great therapy, isn't it?'

Tony leaned towards her and grasped her hands tightly. 'You mean you're ready to come back to work?'

She nodded, her eyes shining.

'But how? When? I mean . . . how did you get over your hang-ups?'

Haltingly, she explained how she'd gone riding to avoid the insurance agent. She didn't tell him about Talan's passionate kiss or Sonia's reaction to it, which had prompted her wild ride, saying only that she had tried to gallop and found that she could.

'It was if I'd never stopped,' she concluded.

Tony's eyes glowed with excitement. 'Then coming here has done you some good after all.'

'I suppose so.' If you only counted the physical benefits, and not the cost of her emotions.

'That's fantastic. The best news. Julie will be thrilled when I tell her. We've all been so worried about you since . . .' He tailed off.

'Since the accident when Terry was killed,' she supplied, her voice strong and unwavering. 'See—I can even face up to it, now, instead of avoiding it and making myself into an emotional cripple.'

'I'm glad, Josie. Does this mean you're ready to go back to work or will you still need more time?'

'I need some time to get myself back into shape but that's all,' she explained, sensing that he was leading up to something. 'Why do you ask?'

'It's just that, well, I might have something that could interest you,' he said awkwardly.

'So this wasn't just a social call after all?'

He grinned sheepishly. 'I was filming in the area, but a producer-friend of mine in Melbourne did mention that if I saw you, I could make you a proposition.'

She affected a sigh of resignation. 'In that case, you'd better tell me about it.'

Needing no further encouragement, he did so. The forthcoming film was an action-adventure story set in the time of the bushrangers. 'So there are lots of wild chases, cliff jumps and shoot-outs. They need you to double for the girlfriend of the leading bushranger. Apparently, she's some sort of society girl who falls in love with him and goes out on his escapades with him, returning to her respectable life in between times.'

'It sounds like fun,' Joselin observed, her excitement building as she visualised the large amount of stunt work such a storyline would entail.

'Then you'll do it?'

'I'll have to talk to my agent about the details, but—yes, you can tell your producer that I've agreed in principle.'

Tony leaned across the table and squeezed her upper arms. 'Good girl! Somehow, I knew this was your picture.'

'Which reminds me,' she said. 'Who's going to play the bushranger?'

Tony grinned. 'Me, of course. Too bad we don't

need stunt women for the kissing scenes.'

She cuffed him playfully. 'Better not let Julie hear you saying that. You'll have to learn to act like a respectably married man.'

He reached into the pocket of his tweed sports coat. 'Speaking of which, I wanted your opinion on something.' He pulled out a ring box and opened it to reveal a wide white-gold wedding band, set with a shallow wave pattern of tiny diamonds. 'Do you think she'll approve of this?'

She took the ring and held it up to the light. 'It's lovely. But isn't it a bit late to be asking, when you've already had it engraved?' On the inside face was written 'To Julie with eternal love from Tony'.

'You're right, I was just seeking reassurance.'

'If the rest of the Aussie film industry could hear the redoubtable Tony Briar saying that, they'd fall about laughing,' she teased. 'But don't worry, your secret is safe with me.'

'Until the next time you need a favour,' he amended and they both laughed. Then he stood up. 'I'd better be on my way, I don't want to be too late reaching Melbourne.

Joselin's face fell. 'Can't you stay for a meal?'

''Fraid not. Julie's expecting me back tonight.'

Her mouth twisted into a wry grin. 'I can see you've been putting the flat to good use in my absence.'

He was unperturbed. 'While the cat's away . . .'

Her laughter was light and genuine. 'Okay. Have fun, you two mice. Just don't forget to send me an invitation to the wedding.'

Tony dropped a kiss on her forehead. 'We won't. I think Julie wants you to be bridesmaid or something.'

'As long as it isn't chaperone!' Chatting companionably, they walked back to Tony's car and she watched as he drove away. Seeing him had taken her

mind off her own problems a little at least. Then there
was the job offer which she hugged to herself. What a
difference it would make once she got back to work
and put all this behind her!

In the kitchen, she cleared away the coffee things,
then her eye was attracted to a strip of white paper
half-hidden under a saucer. She picked it up and
smoothed it out.

'To Julie with eternal love from Tony' was written
on it in Tony's handwriting. It must have been his
instructions to the ring engraver, she realised.

Moodily, she stared at the loving message for a long
time, mentally substituting Joselin and Talan for Julie
and Tony. Then she shook herself. What good did it
do to torture herself? She screwed the paper up again
and dropped it back on to the table.

Talan would be back soon and she could tell him
about Pixie's problem. No matter what he thought of
Joselin, he must listen to her about this. But until he
returned, what she needed was some hard physical
activity to take her mind off her problems.

She debated whether to saddle Quicksilver and go
for a ride, then decided it wasn't enough. She
dismissed a spell of exercises for the same reason.
What she really wanted to do was something involving
and physically demanding. She thought back over
Tony's description of the new film. He had mentioned
wild chases, cliff jumps and shoot-outs. Since she
couldn't stage a chase scene or a shoot-out by herself,
that left only a cliff jump—which was exactly what she
felt like doing.

It was so long since she'd prepared for a stunt that
she fumbled like an amateur getting herself dressed.
Most of her body padding she'd left behind in
Melbourne, never dreaming that she'd want to use it
while she was here. But she had brought along a

leather jumpsuit which had a good deal of protection built into the garment. It was designed for performing stunts in which the actress couldn't afford to appear too obviously padded. As she zipped it up, she studied her reflection in the mirror, noting the twin spots of colour which stood out on her cheekbones.

Her heart was racing and her pulses throbbed, but she recognised the symptoms as positive stress—the kind which told her she was fully alert and ready for anything. It was a relief from the draining negative stress which she'd experienced so often in the last few months.

Glancing down at her hands, she slid the wedding and engagement rings off. They didn't really belong to her in any case, and she didn't want to damage them. She slid them into a bedroom drawer to return to Talan later. Then she pulled gauntlet gloves over her hands and straightened, half-expecting a producer to call 'five minutes, Miss Pride'. But there was no movie set waiting for her. This was a personal test—to prove to herself that she really was ready to go back to work.

Finding enough cardboard cartons to make a soft landing for herself was more of a challenge, but she was lucky that Yarrakina's supplies had been delivered only recently, and the packing cases stood empty against a wall in the dry goods store. She loaded several of them into the back of her sports car, then set off towards a spot she'd noticed on her last ride.

The place she had in mind was a rocky outcrop in the middle of the valley. It served as a firewatch station in summer, and from it, one could see the peaceful valley in all directions. She remembered Pixie telling her how the pioneers used to come to this hill to watch for the fires of nomadic aborigines who poached their sheep for food.

The drive took her along a couple of miles of gravel

road, then along a faint trail between mobs of downy sheep. Once, her progress raised a mob of kangaroos and they bounded off in all directions like wind-up toys.

Along the road, she saw white cockatoos, green parrots, ibis and a flight of black ducks in their v-formation, circling a nearby swamp. The birds dispersed, chattering crossly as she reached the foot of the rocky outcrop. Here she had to leave the car and continue on foot.

Her adrenalin was pumping furiously as she unloaded the cartons and started to arrange them at the foot of the cliff. There was just enough of them to make a reasonable landing place. Studying the results, she clucked her tongue in annoyance. It wasn't good enough to simply land on the boxes. It had to look good as well. So she fetched some sprays of greenery and camouflaged the boxes completely, hoping she would still be able to spot her landing place from above.

She had brought along a half-empty wool sack tied at the neck. Dragging it to the edge of the drop, she judged the angle of the fall, checked the wind direction and shoved the sack down on to the cartons below. It landed a little off to the right and she frowned. If it had been her instead of a dummy, she would have gone right off the edge of the landing place.

It wouldn't do. She clambered down the rockface and rescued the dummy, then had another trial run, this time managing to land the sack right in the centre of the cartons. Much better. Watching the sack thud on to the concealed landing place, she was uncomfortably aware that she shouldn't be doing this entirely alone. What if something went wrong? Where were the medical teams, the safety experts who usually stood by when a stunt was being performed?

Nothing was going to go wrong, she told herself

firmly. Those days were behind her now. Besides, she'd done this stunt hundreds of times, and never come to grief. In fact, the only time she'd had any problems with a simple high fall was when she was too scared to go through with it. And that wasn't going to happen this time.

She checked the wind direction once again and took a mental photograph of the landing place. Then she spent a few minutes preparing her breathing and mentally gearing herself up for the jump.

'It's going to be good,' she said aloud. 'This time, I know it's going to work.'

Then she launched herself at the edge of the cliff.

'Joselin, no! Don't do it!'

The masculine voice tugged at the edges of her awareness, almost ruining her aim. But she was too deeply immersed in her task and she ignored the voice, continuing her run-up.

Before she reached the crumbling edge, however, she was felled by a flying tackle from behind. Then she was falling, but not with the controlled impetus of a calculated jump. She was tumbling helplessly over the edge of the cliff and carrying someone else with her.

It was as if everything was happening in slow motion. She was in Talan's arms and together, they were falling over the edge of the cliff. She had time only for a glimpse of his terrified expression and she closed her eyes against the pain she saw there. It was unmistakably for her.

Then time speeded up again and the ground came rushing to meet them. She was dimly aware that they scraped the edge of the landing place, before going off it on to the tangled scrub around it.

She screamed as a searing pain shot through the back of her head. She was dimly aware that Talan was lying on the ground some distance from her, not moving. Lights danced on and off in front of her eyes but she blinked them away and tried to crawl towards Talan. Then the pain in her head became too much and she blacked out altogether.

An eternity later, she became aware of voices reaching her through a grey haze.

'. . . nasty crack on the head. Possible concussion.'

'. . . why do you think she did it?'

'. . . have you read this?'

'My God! She was in love with this guy, wasn't she?'

Talan! Why didn't somebody tell her what had happened to Talan? Everybody seemed worried over this girl and her love life . . . whoever she was.

She tried to tell the voices that she was awake and aware, but something had happened to her voice and she couldn't force the words out. Nor could she get her eyes to focus beyond the greyness which enveloped her.

'. . . hate to think what would have happened if Talan hadn't turned up in time.'

That's it! Keep talking about Talan. At least . . . dear God . . . they weren't talking about him in the past tense? A sob wrenched at her throat and she felt a hand brush her forehead.

'Sssh dear. You're safe now,' a soothing voice murmured. She didn't recognise it. Then came a man's voice and her heart constricted at the sound of it.

'How is she?'

'Should you be up and about?'

'It's only a bruised rib. Don't fuss.'

He was all right. Thank God, he was all right. She felt a tear squeeze its way past her closed eyelid and slide down her cheek.

Only then, she thought to wonder why she should care so much about this particular man when she had never met him before in her life.

CHAPTER EIGHT

THE room swam slowly into focus as Joselin lifted a fringe of lashes away from her eyes. At first she thought she was still dreaming, because nothing in the room seemed familiar, including the woman in the starched white coat who was rummaging in a black bag. Only when the woman touched a gentle hand to Joselin's forehead, she realised both the room and the woman were real.

'Who are you?' she asked huskily. Her throat felt parched.

'I'm Dr Gordony—Susan Gordony. I've been taking care of you.'

Alarm flickered in the hazel eyes. 'What's wrong with me?'

'Hush. Nothing's wrong with you. You had a bad fall. You were very lucky. Somehow or other, you landed well—instinct I suppose—so you only sustained some bruising and the bump on the back of your head which knocked you out.'

'How long have I been unconscious?'

The doctor frowned. 'A few hours. But then you slept normally for almost twenty-four hours after that. Do you remember much about the accident?'

Tears sprang to Joselin's eyes and she blinked them away. 'I can't remember anything.'

Dr Gordony gripped her hand reassuringly. 'Don't worry. It's usual for the mind to blank out unpleasant details, such as a traumatic accident.'

Joselin shook her head violently. 'No, I mean I can't remember anything—literally.' She closed her eyes and held tightly to the doctor's hand. 'I don't even know who I am ... where I am ... nothing!' Never had she been so frightened in her life as she was of this terrible black void where her past should be.

Sensing her terror, the doctor laid a hand on her forehead. 'It's all right, Joselin. It's all right. You're quite safe here.'

'Joselin? Is that my name?'

'That's right. Joselin Pride. And "here" is a sheep station called Yarrakina. It belonged to your aunt, Pixie Pride, until she sold it to Talan Devereaux.'

The names meant nothing to her—all except one. Talan Devereaux. Talan Devereaux. She said it over and over in her mind, savouring its sweet sound. The name felt as if it should mean something special. 'Talan Devereaux?' she tried it for size. Even saying it aloud made her feel better.

'Your aunt's godson. You practically grew up together since both of you spent a lot of your school holidays here.'

Joselin turned her head aside in anguish. 'Then why can't I remember?'

'You will, given time. Temporary amnesia isn't uncommon after an accident like the one you had. Your memory should return of its own accord.'

'How long will it take?'

The doctor shrugged. 'A few hours or a few days. There have been longer cases documented, but usually total memory loss is only short-term, although you may never regain recall of the events leading up to the accident.' She stood up and began packing her bag. 'All the same, I'm going to have you admitted to hospital for observation and a few tests, just to make sure there's no hidden damage.'

The prospect of being taken away from this tenuous haven filled Joselin with panic. Here, she was among friends, even if she couldn't remember them. And here, also, was a man called Talan Devereaux who meant something important to her, if only she could think what it was.

'No, I don't want to go,' she said tremulously. 'Please, can't I stay here at least until I remember something?'

Susan Gordony looked sympathetic but dubious. 'I really think you should be in hospital.'

'Tal ... Talan can call you if anything goes wrong, can't he? He won't mind me staying, I'm sure he won't.' How she was sure, she didn't know but the certainty was strong.

Biting her lip, the doctor sat down on the edge of the bed again. 'Well, if you really don't want to go, I can't make you even though I strongly recommend it. But ... I suppose Talan can keep an eye on you. I'll ask him and see what he thinks.'

'Ask me what?' came a guardedly cheerful voice.

At the voice, a childlike sensation of relief overcame Joselin. Somehow, she knew without being told, that the tall, commanding man in the doorway was Talan Devereaux. At the same time, she realised with a shock that his left arm was supported in a sling, and his mahogany tan was marred by a violet bruise down one side of his face.

'I can't convince Joselin that she should be in hospital,' the doctor admitted. 'She wants to stay here with you.'

'Is she in any danger if she does?'

'No, not unless there are complications. But I can tell you what to watch for and you can call me at the first sign of trouble.'

Talan grinned. 'Then what's the problem?'

Dr Gordony looked across at Joselin then back to Talan. 'She appears to be suffering from hysterical amnesia. I had to tell her who she is and what happened.'

The colour drained from Talan's face, leaving the bruise standing out in stark relief. 'Can you remember who I am?'

'You're Talan Devereaux,' she said slowly. 'Dr Gordony mentioned the name to me a moment ago. I don't know how I knew it was you, but I did.'

'You're right, of course, and that's a good sign that the amnesia will be temporary,' the doctor said briskly. 'After all, Talan is your . . .'

'Your friend,' he cut in rudely, not giving the doctor a chance to finish. She looked at him curiously, but did not contradict his brusque statement. 'I'd rather she remembered in her own time,' he said in an aside to the doctor.

Remember what? Joselin wondered fearfully. What had the doctor been about to tell her concerning Talan? She already knew he was important to her. That feeling went deeper than conscious knowledge. Surely that meant there was more than mere friendship between them?

She watched as he escorted the doctor to the bedroom door and strained to hear the words they exchanged when they reached the landing, but couldn't catch any of it. The doctor was probably telling Talan what symptoms to watch for, she decided.

Her heart leapt as Talan came back into the room and her smile was dazzling, but it faded when she saw the melancholy way he was looking at her. 'What's the matter?' she asked uncertainly. 'Was there something the doctor didn't tell me?'

'Actually, it was something I didn't tell her,' he said cryptically. 'But we can discuss all that later. For now, you need rest and quiet.'

'Will you stay a while?' she asked tremulously.

'No, I can't,' he said as if the words were being forced out of him. 'I have to go to town to visit Pixie. She'll worry if none of us come to see her.'

She wrinkled her brow with concentration. 'Pixie. She's my aunt, and the former owner of this property, isn't she?'

'That's right. Susan must have told you. Did she also mention that Pixie's in hospital, recovering from heart surgery?'

'No! Is she all right?'

'Yes, thank goodness. But she mustn't be bothered by anything stressful for a while.'

'Like my accident?' she asked ruefully.

He nodded agreement. 'I'm afraid so. If I told her that you'd knocked yourself cold and lost your memory, she'd worry herself into a relapse.'

'What will you tell her then?'

He rubbed his chin thoughtfully with his undamaged hand. 'I'll say you were called back to Melbourne for an audition. She'll understand that.'

Her eyes went round. 'An audition? Does that mean I'm some sort of actress?'

'So I'm told. We haven't discussed your work very much since you came here.'

Something in his tone alerted her. 'You don't approve of what I do?'

'Maybe not. Let's say I don't approve of the type of woman your world seems to attract. I prefer my women to be warm and genuine, not the fickle, manipulative type.'

Like me? she wondered. Was that the sort of woman she was? Somehow, she didn't care for the idea. She decided on a change of subject. 'Won't Pixie be alarmed by your injuries?' she asked.

He waved the sling at her. 'You mean this? I'll take

it off before I go in to see her. The wrist is only sprained, not broken. Susan says I can get rid of the support altogether in a day or so.' He rubbed the bruised side of his face reflectively. 'I won't be able to hide this quite so easily, though.'

'You can tell her you tangled with a wild creature,' she suggested.

He regarded her thoughtfully. 'It wouldn't be much of a lie, either.'

She took a deep breath and let it out slowly. 'Did you get hurt in the same accident as mine?'

'You could say that.' It was obvious that he didn't intend to elaborate on this, for he moved towards the door. 'I have to go now. You get some rest.'

At the doorway, he turned. 'My housekeeper and her family are all away right now, worst luck. But our neighbour, Sonia Hall, is staying with us so she'll make sure you're looked after. Call her if you need anything.'

She smiled wanly at him. 'Thanks, I will. Give . . . give my love to Pixie.'

Then he was gone and she was alone in the unfamiliar room. Why was he so reluctant to tell her how they came by their injuries? And what information had he kept from the doctor?

If only she could remember!

For the next half-hour she tried to explore every corner of her mind, seeking some clue to who and what she had been before the accident. But it was as if someone had drawn a misty veil over everything before the moment when she awoke in this room. Soon her head ached with the effort, and she closed her eyes miserably.

She opened them again when there came a light tap on her door. It opened and woman's face appeared around it. 'Oh good, you're awake, I brought you some lunch.'

'That was kind of you,' she said as the woman settled a tray across her knees. 'You must be Sonia.'

The woman's eyebrows lifted. 'Was that a lucky guess or did Talan tell you?'

Joselin smiled gently. 'Process of elimination, really. Talan said you were staying here. His housekeeper has gone away, and he didn't mention anyone else.'

'How clever of you,' Sonia said in a patronising tone which made the fine hairs on the back of Joselin's neck lift slightly. There was no reason for thinking it, but she had the feeling she and Sonia didn't get along very well.

Her hunch was soon confirmed. Sonia solicitously poured a cup of tea for Joselin from a silver pot on the tray, then uncovered a plate of asparagus sandwiches. As Joselin took a bite, she said coolly, 'Talan tells me you don't remember trying to kill yourself.'

Choking on a mouthful of sandwich, Joselin pushed the plate away. 'I did *what*?'

'You tried to throw yourself off a cliff because you found out that your boyfriend was in love with someone else.' From a pocket in her fashionable shirtwaister, she pulled out a crumpled slip of paper, smoothed it out and handed it to Joselin. 'We found this on the kitchen table after you were brought back here. It explains a lot.'

The message on the paper said 'To Julie with eternal love from Tony'. Neither of the names meant anything to Joselin. 'Is . . . I mean was this Tony my boyfriend?'

'He sure was. You were wearing his ring when you arrived. Here, put it on. Maybe wearing it will help you to remember.'

Numbly, Joselin accepted the ring which Sonia proffered. The sight of it should have awakened memories of love given and received, but she felt

unmoved as she stared at the sapphire and silver jewel
in the palm of her hand. Experimentally, she slipped it
on to the third finger of her right hand. It went over
her knuckle with an effort. Whoever had chosen it
didn't know her ring size very well.

Sonia watched her impassively. 'How does it feel?'

'Strange,' Joselin answered frankly. 'It doesn't feel
like my ring at all.'

'Give it time,' Sonia urged. 'You had a nasty crack
on the head. If Talan hadn't . . .' She stopped, her
expression guilty.

'Please, tell me the rest,' urged Joselin. 'Nobody
else will.'

Sonia made a show of appearing reluctant. 'In that
case, maybe I shouldn't either.'

'Look, you've told me this much. At least tell me
where Talan comes into the picture.'

Sonia gave a martyred sigh. 'Very well, but only
because you insist. Talan came back just as you were
about to hurl yourself off a cliff. He stopped you and
injured himself in the process. My fiancé's like that—
forever rescuing strays from danger.'

Recalling the childish maxim about sticks and
stones, Joselin couldn't believe that words could inflict
such pain as she felt listening to Sonia. So she was no
more than a stray Talan had rescued from her own
folly.

'You said Talan's your fiancé?' she whispered.

Coyly, Sonia nodded. 'It isn't official yet, but it's
only a matter of time. In fact, we would probably have
made the announcement this weekend if you
hadn't . . .' She smiled apologetically at Joselin. 'But I
shouldn't blame you though, should I? Of all people, I
should know what wild impetuous things one can do
for love.'

Since Sonia looked neither wild, nor impetuous,

Joselin doubted this very much but she held her tongue. It seemed she had already caused enough trouble by her actions, so she had no right to criticise anyone else. 'I still don't understand why I'm here,' she ventured, anxious to leave the subject of Talan for the moment. 'The doctor tells me my aunt no longer owns this property.'

'She's right. Talan bought Yarrakina from your aunt when she became too ill to keep it up. It seems nobody told you until you turned up here expecting to be able to stay. Talan agreed to let you—although he's probably regretting it now, but since you had nowhere else to go, we didn't have much choice except to put you up.'

Wincing inwardly, Joselin looked away. It didn't sound as though she was very welcome at Yarrakina. Maybe she should have let the doctor take her away to hospital after all. 'Why did I come here?' she asked.

Sonia shrugged expressively. 'Who knows? You had some sort of story about needing a holiday but my guess was, you knew about the sale all along and you couldn't resist sizing up the new owner.'

'Sizing him up? I don't understand.'

Eyes gleaming, Sonia smiled mirthlessly. 'Don't you? Come on, Joselin, we both know the score. When an eligible bachelor takes over a property like Yarrakina, it stands to reason he's going to need a helpmate. Your relationship with this Tony character was already shaky—who could blame you for seeking greener pastures?'

Joselin stared at Sonia in amazement, hardly believing that anyone could have such a devious mind. 'I think you're wrong about my motives,' she said stiffly. 'I may not remember why I came here, but I'm sure it isn't for the reasons you've suggested.'

'I'll bet,' Sonia said drily.

Ignoring the interruption, Joselin went on, 'In any case, I can see that I've already imposed on you quite enough, so I'll be on my way as soon as the doctor allows it.'

Sonia looked at her for a long moment then tossed her auburn hair in a careless gesture. In a voice pitched just low enough for Joselin to catch, she said, 'You can say that again.' Then she flounced out of the room.

Alone again, Joselin took a half-hearted bite of the asparagus sandwich she'd started, then returned it to the plate. Her appetite had been completely destroyed by Sonia's remarks. Could she really have come to Yarrakina to 'size up' Talan as a prospective husband? The idea seemed possible of a woman like Sonia—even probably—but search her soul as she might, Joselin couldn't believe she would do such a thing herself.

With a heavy sigh, she placed the tray on the bedside table and rolled over on to her side, cradling her head on one arm, and bringing the other around so she could look at the ring Sonia had brought to her. It looked alien on her finger. Closing her eyes she tried to conjure up a mental picture of the man who had supposedly given it to her. Tony, Sonia said his name was. Tony who? She had a fleeting impression of a boyishly handsome face, then the image faded. Was this the man she had loved enough to try to kill herself over?

At least she understood now why Talan hadn't told the doctor the whole story about the accident. If he had, Dr Gordony would have insisted on taking Joselin to the hospital—for psychiatric help as well.

As she lay there with her eyes closed, another face imposed itself over the first one. This one she could easily picture in graphic detail—from the piercing blue-black eyes shaded by bushy brows, to the high-bridged and slightly uneven nose which gave his face such character. The jaw was strong and firm, shadowed a little as if he needed to shave twice a day. Then she recalled the disfiguring bruise down one side of his face and she shuddered. To think he had acquired his injuries saving her from a suicidal leap.

A sob shook her slender frame and she turned her head into the pillow to muffle it, not wanting to attract Sonia's attention. She wasn't even sure why she was crying. Was it self-pity, for her own sorry love life; or was it a deeper sorrow—for the end of a relationship which, according to Sonia, had never properly begun?

In this despairing frame of mind, she drifted into a troubled sleep, giving herself up to it willingly to escape from the painful realities of wakefulness.

She knew he was in the room even before she opened her eyes. In drawing a veil over her memories, her mind seemed to have sharpened her senses to keener awareness, so she felt his presence even before it was confirmed by the musky scent of his after-shave lotion and the characteristic rhythm of his breathing.

She opened her eyes slowly, drinking in the sight of him as if it was a tonic for her ills. 'Hello, Talan.'

His gaze which had been caressing when first she opened her eyes, became shuttered so she couldn't tell what he was thinking. Perhaps he realised he was being disloyal to Sonia by looking at another woman that way. 'Hello, little one,' he said softly. 'Did you sleep well?'

How long had he been keeping watch over her? 'Yes thank you.' She couldn't tell him that her dreams had been peopled by the two of them, walking and talking companionably as if Sonia didn't exist. She felt her colour rise as she remembered the way he had embraced her in the dream, and she said quickly, 'How was Aunt Pixie?'

'Recovering nicely, the doctor tells me. He seems worried about her, though. He said her recovery's being hampered by the uncertainty of her future. As if I would let her live anywhere but here!'

'Does she know that?' Joselin asked instinctively.

Talan looked thoughtful. 'Maybe she doesn't. I just assumed that she would come here, and I assumed she knew it too. This is her home and always will be, no matter whose name is on the title deed—and I'll make sure she understands that the next time I see her.'

'Are you discussing Pixie?' Sonia asked, coming into the room.

Joselin tensed at the sight of her, but Talan accepted her presence easily. 'I was telling Joselin that Pixie seems to think she can't live here after she's discharged from the hospital. I never thought to discuss it with her, taking it for granted that this was her home. But perhaps because I said nothing, she acquired the idea that she isn't welcome here any more.'

'I know you feel that way, but are you sure it's best for Pixie?' Sonia queried, her face a study in concern for the elderly woman. 'Shouldn't she be closer to medical help in case she has problems in future?'

Talan eyed Sonia sharply. 'I hope you didn't put that idea in Pixie's head?'

'Of course not. I'm just pointing out the facts—she is getting on, and we're a long way from a hospital if anything goes wrong in future.'

'Nothing will go wrong,' Talan said firmly. 'We can always get a doctor out here if need be. After all, she lived here alone for the last twenty years—didn't she, Joselin?'

Sonia shot Joselin a venomous look, as if blaming

her for the turn the conversation had taken. 'How would she know?' she demanded. 'She can't even remember her own name.'

'Granted,' Talan said smoothly, 'but she will in time. In any case, I'm sure she remembers most things on an unconscious level, if not consciously—don't you, Joselin?'

Was that why she felt such an inexplicable bond with Talan—based on some unconscious knowledge she was presently unable to tap? 'I suppose so,' she sighed. 'I just wish I could bring it to the surface.'

'Give it time,' Talan reiterated. 'Luckily Pixie accepted my explanation about you being called back to Melbourne so she won't expect to see you for a few days. By then, you'll probably remember everything.'

Sonia rubbed her hands together impatiently. 'I came to tell you that dinner's ready, Talan.'

'What about Joselin?'

'I'll bring hers in on a tray,' she said dismissively.

Joselin started to push back the bedcovers. 'There's no need to wait on me, Sonia. I can come down and eat in the dining room.'

Suddenly, Sonia was all concern. She replaced the covers firmly over Joselin and smiled in a way which didn't quite reach her eyes. 'There's no need for that, dear. I don't mind bringing something up. We want you to get well, after all.'

And well away from here, was the unspoken message Joselin received. Resignedly, she lay back against the pillows, picturing Sonia and Talan sharing their meal downstairs.

When her meal was brought up, it was Talan and not Sonia who carried the tray in and set it at her bedside. The smell of home-made cauliflower soup and crusty bread with a bubbling layer of grilled cheese on top tantalised her nostrils.

'Should you be carrying things with your injured wrist?' she asked anxiously.

He picked up her untouched lunch tray, frowning at the amount of food still on it. 'Don't worry about me,' he instructed. 'I'm pretty well indestructible.'

As he was about to leave, she felt an urge to restrain him, to keep the warmth of his presence with her for just a little longer. 'Talan . . .' she began.

He paused at the door. 'Yes?'

'I just wanted to say thank you for . . . for everything,' she finished lamely. She had wanted to say thanks for saving my life, but she couldn't bring herself to say it. She had only Sonia's explanation for what happened.

The sorrowful look returned to his face. 'I'm not sure you should be thanking me after the mess I've made of your life,' he said cryptically, and closed the door between them.

What did he mean by that? she wondered as she slowly spooned soup from the bowl. Maybe he had something to do with the end of her love affair with the mysterious Tony. Had Talan tried to make love to her, somehow coming between her and her boyfriend? she wondered.

Was that why his expression was one of tenderness mixed with regret when he looked at her? It was the only thing she could think of to explain all the pieces of the puzzle. It would also explain why Sonia was so antagonistic towards her.

Impatiently, she dropped the spoon into the bowl, heedless of the soup which splashed on to the tray. Could she be capable of accepting one man's ring and dallying with another? Sonia seemed to think so. But what sort of woman did it make her if it was true?

As she lay back against the pillows, her head was in a whirl. If only she could remember something of her life before the accident! Until then, she was forced to accept Sonia's view that she was an unscrupulous man-chaser. It seemed Joselin had already tried to come between Talan and Sonia. Thank God she hadn't succeeded. But she had apparently succeeded in ruining her own relationship with this Tony. The sooner she recovered enough to get out of here the better—before she did any more harm.

But time didn't seem to help matters any. Two days later, she was well enough to pitch in and help with the running of the house but she was still no closer to recovering her memory.

Talan protested that she was doing too much but Sonia, predictably, encouraged her to do as many of the chores as she liked. 'It will help keep your mind off your problems,' she said acidly. Unless Talan was around, she no longer bothered to conceal her dislike of Joselin.

For Joselin's part, she was quite happy to help with the household chores and the cooking. Although she was quite capable of doing both, Sonia made it clear she preferred to leave those activities to someone else while she acted the lady of the house, concocting gourmet evening meals to impress Talan, while leaving the plain cooking to Joselin. She was entitled to, Joselin supposed, since it wouldn't be long before she was mistress of Yarrakina, as Talan's wife.

'Will you be back in time for dinner?' she asked as Sonia prepared to accompany Talan to Stawell to visit Pixie. From being reluctant to visit the elderly lady, Sonia had become positively enthusiastic about it—as an excuse to have Talan to herself, Joselin supposed.

'There's no need for you to do all the work—we can do our share when we get back,' Talan insisted.

Joselin smiled at him. 'It's all right. I made a batch of casseroles and pastries yesterday, so I only have to heat them up.'

His hand reached out and froze in mid-air, in line with her cheek. Joselin was sure he was about to caress her. Then he dropped the hand to his side. 'Just don't work too hard. You're still a semi-invalid yourself,' he said brusquely.

Sonia shuffled her feet impatiently. 'Come on, Talan, or we'll miss visiting hours.'

Joselin was relieved when they had gone. In Sonia's presence she felt like a cross between Cinderella and the Scarlet Woman. But until her memory returned, she had no defence against Sonia's accusations.

To distract herself from thinking too much, she began dusting the large living room, finding solace in the physical activity. She was absorbed in cleaning the intricate marble fireplace surrounds when the doorbell pealed. The door was ajar and through it came a cheerful male voice. 'Anyone home?'

'In here,' she called and got to her feet. When she went into the hall, a man was standing there smiling at her. She looked at him uncertainly, feeling that she should know him.

The man took her hand. 'It's all right, Joselin, I heard about your accident and I know you can't remember me right now. I'm Tony Briar.'

She tore her hand from his grasp as if burnt. '*You're* Tony?' she asked, her voice rising in pitch. 'You're the one who's in love with Julie.'

The man laughed. 'Shouldn't I be?'

Joselin clutched her hands to the sides of her head. 'I'm sorry. Things are a bit mixed up right now. Come into the living room and maybe you can help me get a few things straight.'

'That's why I came,' Tony said, as he followed her into the living room.

Distractedly, she apologised for the cleaning things still cluttering the floor, but he dismissed her apologies. 'I came to see if I could help you remember,' Tony said anxiously. 'I've rung your friend Talan a few times, but he can't—or won't—tell me what happened.'

At least she knew one thing which *hadn't* happened—she had never tried to kill herself over this man. All she felt towards him was warmth and friendliness. Surely if he'd deserted her, she would feel something quite different towards him?

They talked for a while about people whom Joselin apparently knew well, but couldn't remember. None of it seemed to help. At last, Joselin decided to take the bull by the horns.

'Tony—have we ever been ... well ... more than just friends?'

He looked startled by the question. 'You mean were we lovers? No, we weren't. I wanted to take you out but you refused because you said it was too risky for two people in our industry to share a life, so it was better not to start something we couldn't finish. Then you introduced me to your flatmate, Julie, and well, there was nobody else for me after that. Are you disappointed?'

Her glowing expression revealed anything but disappointment. 'No, I'm relieved,' she said, baffling him. She still didn't know why Sonia had said she and Tony had been engaged. Perhaps she'd got her wires crossed and mistaken Joselin for Julie, she thought charitably.

Her eye was drawn to the sapphire ring on her finger and she twisted it off, holding it out to Tony. 'Then you didn't give me this?'

He looked at it and shook his head. 'I never saw it before in my life.'

Curiouser and curiouser, she thought, dropping the ring on to a side table. Whatever Sonia was up to, it wasn't designed to help Joselin, she felt sure now. She couldn't even rely on Sonia's implication that Joselin had tried to come between her and Talan. Maybe it was the other way around—perhaps Talen had made the advances, bringing Sonia's wrath down on them both. It would explain the tender looks and half-gestures Talan kept making towards Joselin. Perplexed, she rested her head in her hands.

At once, Tony was anxious. 'I hope I did the right thing in coming here. I only wanted to help.'

She looked up at him through pain-filled eyes. 'It's all right, Tony. You have helped, more than you know. It's just so frustrating that I can't remember anything. It's like having pieces of a puzzle but no idea what the finished picture looks like.'

Tony stood up. 'I'd better leave. I don't want to tire you out.'

'Please don't go yet,' she begged. 'I feel if I only keep trying, it will all come back.'

'All the same, I think I should go,' Tony repeated. 'I can stay in a motel in Stawell for a day or so, and come back again if you need me.'

'I doubt whether Joselin will need anything from you,' interrupted an angry male voice. They looked up to see Talan standing in the doorway, his face dark with barely leashed fury.

Tony stepped forward and held out his hand. 'Good to see you again, Talan. I came to see if I could help Joselin in any way.'

'You can best help by getting the hell out of here,' Talan growled. 'Don't you think you've done enough harm around here?'

Tony looked helplessly at Joselin. 'What did I do?' Then his face cleared. 'I get it, you're still mad over what Joselin and I did, aren't you?'

'I don't know how you dare show your face around here,' Talan said furiously.

'Look, it was only a harmless bit of fun.'

'Is that what you call it? Where Joselin's concerned, I don't find it the least bit funny.'

Talan must still think that Tony threw her over for Julie, Joselin realised. Quickly, she stepped between them. 'Talan, there's no need to act like this. It wasn't Tony's fault. The truth is . . .'

Talan was staring at her in amazement. 'You can still defend him after everything that's happened?'

With pantherlike grace, he moved towards Tony but Joselin held her ground between them. 'I think you'd better go,' she said to Tony over her shoulder.

He spread his hands wide. 'Sure, sure. I didn't come here looking for trouble.' As he moved cautiously past Talan, he said, 'I've heard a lot about country hospitality, but this takes the cake.'

'Get out of here,' Talan repeated dangerously.

'I'm sorry, Tony,' Joselin began but he silenced her with a reassuring smile. 'It's okay, kid. At least I don't have to worry about you having someone to take care of you.' He looked back at Talan, still braced in the doorway, his hands balled into fists. 'You've got a real champion there. I'm glad I don't have to fight him for your hand.'

Still shaken by the sudden turn of events, she waited while Tony drove away then marshalled her reserves of courage and went back inside. Champion or not, Talan Devereaux needed straightening out on a few things.

CHAPTER NINE

HE was still standing in the doorway so she had to duck under his arm to get into the room. As she did so, he dropped the arm around her shoulders and pulled her hard against him.

'What are you doing?' she demanded, thrown off guard. At his touch, her body began to respond quite independently of her will. She felt her temperature rise and her face flood with colour. In vain, she tried to twist free.

'So it's good enough for Tony, but not for me,' he said in an ugly tone.

'Tony came to see how I was, no more and no less,' she spat out through clenched teeth.

'I'd call it having his cake and eating it,' he countered, propelling her forcibly into the room. For a moment, she thought he was going to kiss her but he deposited her unceremoniously on the couch and dropped into the opposite one, resting his head in his hands. 'Hell, I'm sorry. I shouldn't have flown off the handle like that, but when I saw him here, I just saw red.'

Free of his touch, she felt her composure returning. 'You thought I'd swallowed my pride and accepted him back,' she said evenly. 'Well, it wasn't like that at all. Tony means nothing to me and never did.'

He brought his head up. 'There's no need to be brave about it. Bottling things up never does any good and he just isn't worth it. He was the one who got you into this fix, remember?'

Astonished, she stared at him. 'In the first place, I

can't remember as you very well know. And in the
second place, if you blame Tony for burdening you
with me—why don't you come right out and say it?'

'Now just a minute!'

But she wasn't waiting around for any more of his
explanations. She'd had enough. In a fury, she raced
up the stairs to her room and hauled her suitcase out
from under the bed. Opening it on the bed, she began
to pile clothes into it anyhow.

'Where do you think you're going?'

She tensed, realising that he had followed her up the
stairs. 'Anywhere, as long as it's away from you,' she
snapped, continuing to fill the suitcase.

He moved up behind her and placed both hands on
her shoulders, turning her to face him. 'Don't go—
please?' he said huskily.

'I thought you'd be glad to get rid of me,' she
rejoined, remembering his comments downstairs.

'Oh no, never that.'

'But what about Sonia?'

He frowned. 'Sonia has nothing to do with this.'

How lightly he must take his relationships if he
could say that—and he accused Tony of trying to have
his cake and eat it! Obviously, he was speaking from
experience. She wrenched herself free of his grasp and
continued with her packing.

Suddenly a lace-frilled underslip went flying past
her ear and she whirled around. Talan was taking
things out of her case as fast as she could put them in.

She ducked as a bra went sailing across the room.
'Hey, cut that out!'

'When you agree to stay.'

'No!'

At once, a pair of stockings went flying, followed by
her silk shirt. She grabbed at them and missed so they
landed in a heap in a corner of the room. Had he gone

mad? Then she caught the gleam of anger in his eyes and realised that he was deadly serious. There was no way she was getting her suitcase packed tonight.

In apparent defeat, she slumped on the bed. Maybe if she pretended to give in, she could pack and leave later while he was busy or asleep. 'All right, you win.'

He looked at her suspiciously. 'You promise to stay?'

'I said you'd won, didn't I?'

Whisking a flimsy black lace bra from her case, he held it aloft. 'Not good enough. I need your word.'

Squealing, she made a grab for it. How dare he handle her things so . . . so possessively? But he was quicker. Evading her outstretched hand, he hurled the bra up into the air so it tangled around the light fixture and dangled there like a war pennant. 'You're despicable!' she fumed.

He grinned. 'And you're fascinating. Who'd ever have guessed that such an outwardly prim creature possessed such a wanton streak as these—garments—suggest.'

'What makes you think that the wanton creature isn't the real me?' she couldn't resist asking. 'I don't know who I am really, so how can you?'

'I know very well who you are, Joselin Pride,' he said, suddenly serious. 'I'm beginning to think you're that worst of all manipulating women—a tease.'

'Why . . . why do you say that?'

'You may not remember, but you've done nothing but lead me on since you got here. I'll bet you even invited those other men here to provoke me—Tony Briar and that Wizzard fellow from Melbourne.'

'Since I don't know what you're talking about, I can't confirm or deny it so that gives you the upper hand,' she said tiredly.

His mouth twisted into a sneer. 'I've never had the

upper hand with you since you were twelve. And especially not now. You led me on with no intention of ever letting me make love to you, didn't you?'

She was still sprawled in an undignified position across the bed and she drew her legs slowly up beneath her, unconsciously curling herself into a tight, defensive ball. 'Get out of here, I hate you,' she hissed. 'I can't believe you're being so cruel.'

'So I'm the one who's cruel now, am I? What about when you put me through hell with wanting you, and always managed to escape at the last moment?'

'You make it sound as though we had quite an affair,' she said coldly.

His eyes raked her from head to curled-up toes. 'Oh we did, lady, we sure did.' With that, he turned on his heel and left, slamming the bedroom door behind him.

For several minutes, she remained in the bed staring after him, half-hoping he would come back and say he hadn't meant any of the cruel things he'd said. Was it true? Had she been such a tease, leading him on then reneging at the last moment?

It fitted Sonia's description of Joselin as an unscrupulous man-chaser. And it also explained why Sonia was so hostile. She would be, too, if Talan belonged to her and another woman tried to come between them.

Clutching a hand to her mouth, she stifled a sob. He hadn't even given her a chance to tell him that she and Tony had never been lovers. Would it make any difference if he knew? Probably not. He would still think she had invited Tony here for some manipulative game of her own.

Despondently, she surveyed the wreckage of the room. Her clothes were strewn from one end of the carpet to the other, making it look as if some highly selective snowstorm had blown through. Mechanically, she began to collect her things, folding them and replacing them in the suitcase. Talan hadn't managed to extract a promise that she would stay, so she was free to carry out her plan to leave later tonight.

When she had finished, she tiptoed to the door and tried the handle, intending to peep out and see whether Talan was around. To her annoyance, the door refused to budge.

'He wouldn't!' she said.

But it seemed he would. Talan had not only locked her door from the outside, he had taken away the key so there was no trick she could use to let herself out.

She debated the wisdom of screaming the place down, but decided against it. She wasn't sure how many people knew about her so-called suicide attempt and she didn't want them thinking she had finally cracked altogether.

So what was she going to do?

Looking upwards, she caught sight of the black bra hanging from the light fitting. It looked so absurd there that she began to laugh and, having started, she was unable to stop. Soon, she was rolling on the bed with helpless mirth.

There was a sharp rap on the door. 'Joselin, are you all right?'

She recognised Talan's voice but she was too convulsed with laughter to answer him. A moment later, the door crashed open and he stood looking down at her.

Then he slid an arm under her shoulders and pulled her upright. It was only when he drew his arm back that she realised what he had in mind. 'Don't,' she gasped through tears of laughter, 'I'm not hysterical, honestly.'

'Then why didn't you answer me?' he demanded.

'I ... I ... oh, it was too f-f-funny,' she choked, beginning to laugh again.

A smile twitched at the corners of his mouth. 'For goodness' sake tell me what's so amusing.'

Unable to get the words out, she pointed at the bra hanging from the ceiling, swaying gently in the breeze stirred up by their movements.

'Your cup runneth over,' he said drily. 'All right, I can see the funny side of it, I suppose.'

'M-me packing and you unp-packing as fast as you could,' she gasped, remembering.

Then he began to chuckle too. 'All right, it was funny, now you come to mention it.'

His arm was still around her and as they laughed, he lowered her back against the pillows so they lay side by side on top of the bedclothes, rocking with shared laughter.

They turned their heads at the same moment and their noses collided, causing a further ripple of merriment. But it was soon stilled as his lips came into contact with hers. The contact was so unexpected and so thrilling that her laughter died stillborn. 'Oh, Talan,' she whispered. 'We ... we shouldn't ...'

It was a feeble protest because every nerve in her body urged him to continue. Through her clothes, Joselin felt the searing heat generated by his passion as he covered her face with tiny kisses. She moved her head until their lips met and they feasted on each other hungrily.

She was aware of a thousand sensations all crowding in on her at once. The fiery heat of his lips on hers. The musky scent of his after-shave lotion, mixed with faint sheep-farm odours and an indefinable male essence which tugged at her senses. The sinewy hardness of the thigh he had thrown over her legs, imprisoning them. She felt as if she was going to faint from sheer sensory overload, and she clung to him desperately.

Sensing her need, he brought his free arm around her shoulders and pressed his lips against the hollow of her throat. A small moan of longing escaped her lips and she caressed the fading bruise on his cheek.

Through his shirt she could feel the tape wound around his damaged ribs but he seemed oblivious to his injuries, pulling her closer as if their embrace was all that mattered to him.

Only when he began to undo the buttons of her shirt did she start to come to her senses. If she let him undress her, he wouldn't be able to call her a tease any more because there would simply be no stopping him. And until she knew who she was and what they meant to each other, she dared not risk letting him make love to her.

'Talan, no,' she said urgently, struggling to free herself.

At first, caught up in a tide of passion, he resisted, sliding his hands possessively inside her shirt to mould her pliant flesh. His fingers burned her skin and she shuddered with longing.

'I said no,' she repeated more loudly and pulled his hands away, feeling as if she was tearing away some of her own flesh.

Plainly annoyed, he rolled a little away, watching as she buttoned her shirt again. 'What's so wrong with me wanting to make love to you?' he demanded.

'That's just it, I don't know whether it's wrong or not,' she said miserably. 'I'm not a tease, no matter what you think. But I don't know what I mean to you—or even if I mean anything at all. I can't take the risk that this may be just a one-night stand.'

'We could be married, you know,' he said casually.

In a flash, she recalled the doctor saying, 'After all, he is your ...' then being interrupted by Talan, supplying the word 'friend'. 'That isn't funny,' she said tautly. 'We can't possibly be married.'

'Is the prospect so repulsive?'

'It isn't that. There's ... there's Sonia, for one thing.' Sonia who claimed to be Talan's fiancée.

'Why do you keep bringing Sonia into it?' he asked crossly. 'I don't keep throwing Tony at you ... or that other guy who came here looking for you.'

Was it tit for tat then? Had they been having an affair which he blamed Tony for disrupting, turning to Sonia in retaliation? Her head ached with the effort of trying to sort it all out.

Swinging her legs over the side of the bed, she rested her head in her hands. 'Tony—Sonia—you—me—how should I know where we all fit? You insist on talking in riddles and yet you blame me for not understanding.'

Talan rose heavily, tucking his shirt back into his jeans with quick, impatient movements. 'I suppose I'm not being very fair to you,' he agreed. 'I guess I don't know where I fit into your life either. I was hoping you'd remember of your own accord, and then you'd be able to tell me. If you decided never to remember, I didn't want you to feel you owed me anything. I wanted to keep you here so we'd have a chance to work things out.'

'Locking me in my room isn't the way.'

'I'm sorry about that. And about throwing your clothes around. You can leave if you want to. I won't try to stop you.'

He looked so cowed that her heart went out to him. Somehow, she knew it was a rare sight and she didn't feel very proud of having reduced the indomitable Talan Devereaux to such a state.

'I'll give it a few more days,' she said reluctantly. 'But if my memory doesn't return I'll have to go back to Melbourne and see if being in familiar surroundings will help to restore it.'

The relief which lit his eyes reminded her of a light being turned on in a dark room. 'Thank you,' he said simply. At the door, he hesitated, saying diffidently, 'I have one suggestion which might help.'

'What is it?'

'There's a place—a special place, which only a handful of people have ever seen. I ... I took you there soon after we were ... after you arrived. Maybe if we went back there tomorrow ...' He tailed off, as if uncertain of her response.

'Of course I'll go with you,' she said unhesitatingly. 'I don't know what good it will do, but anything is worth a try.'

By unspoken agreement, they didn't mention their plans to Sonia at dinner that night. When she announced her intention to go shopping in Stawell tomorrow, they exchanged secret smiles.

'Would you like to come with me, Joselin?' Sonia asked politely.

Joselin's heart jumped. 'No, thank you,' she said. 'I thought I'd have a look around Yarrakina tomorrow and see if it helps jog my memory.'

Sonia sniffed dubiously. 'I don't know what looking at mobs of sheep will do, but you're welcome to it. You'll come with me though, won't you, Talan?'

'For all the use I'd be choosing women's clothes, you're better off without me,' he said pleasantly, leaving her no avenue for argument. Looking put-out, Sonia was silent throughout the rest of the meal.

After breakfast next day, Talan made himself scarce, saying he had chores to do in the home paddock. Joselin wondered if he had forgotten his promise to take her to his special place.

But he waited just long enough for Sonia to drive away on her shopping trip, before coming back inside. Joselin had finished clearing away the breakfast things and was stacking the dishes in the automatic dishwasher.

'Ready?' he asked.

She dried her hands on a tea towel. 'I wondered if you had forgotten.'

'No, I hadn't forgotten.'

She was already dressed in a yellow western-style shirt with toning mustard jeans tucked into black cowboy boots. 'I hope I'm dressed for the occasion,' she said uncertainly. 'Since you were being so mysterious, I didn't know what to wear.'

He looked her up and down appreciatively. 'You'll do fine. I can't help wondering though . . .'

As he hesitated, she prompted, 'Wondering what?'

'Why you choose such severe clothes to cover up such frivolous underthings?'

Blushing furiously, she hurled the tea towel at him. 'One more word about my underwear and I'll refuse to go anywhere with you.'

He sobered at once. 'Just joking. But you don't know how good it is to see you laughing. That haunted look you've been wearing lately just about breaks my heart.'

'You'd look haunted, too, if you couldn't remember a single thing about your past,' she reminded him.

'Well, let's hope today's outing will be of some use.'

She hoped so too, more than he could ever imagine. Because as long as there was a void where her past should be, she couldn't trust herself with him. Yesterday's kiss was still imprinted on her mouth. Her lips had felt tender and swollen when she cleaned her teeth this morning. And her body still burned in the secret places his hands had wandered.

In that same indefinable way that she knew he meant something important to her, she knew she had never slept with any man before, so they had never been lovers. What had they been to each other? Perhaps today she would find out.

'Won't Pixie miss your visit?' she asked as they saddled their horses for the ride. Although she couldn't recall Quicksilver's name, the horse remembered her and nuzzled her happily when she approached him.

'Sonia's going to call in and see her,' he explained. 'Don't worry, Pixie understands that a sheep station can't be left to run itself so she won't mind me missing one day.'

Yet he was willing to neglect his responsibilities to look after her, she thought guiltily. 'Maybe I shouldn't take up so much of your time,' she ventured. 'If you have other things you should be doing . . .'

'Nothing is more important than getting you well,' he said in a tone which brooked no argument. 'We're having a lull right now, before the shearing season. Then all hell will break loose around here, but for the time being, I have a few days to call my own.'

Satisfied that she wasn't imposing on him, she settled down to enjoy the ride. Discovering that she was at home on a horse was a curious experience. When she tried to concentrate on her task, she was clumsy and awkward but as soon as she relaxed, the movements came automatically. 'At least I know I can ride,' she said with a smile, as they followed a faint trail across a pasture.

'You ride damned well. I watched you a few days ago after you came out to visit the muster camp. You took off like a bat out of hell and rode like the wind.' He looked at her thoughtfully. 'I wonder where you learned to ride like that.'

'Didn't the doctor say I spent most of my school holidays here?' she queried.

'Yes, but in those days you were only capable. From

what I saw, you've turned into a real stunt rider since then.'

She turned her head sharply. 'What makes you say that?'

'I don't know. What was it I said?'

'About me being a stunt rider.'

'Did it trigger something?'

'Yes, but ... it's no use, it's gone again.' His choice of words had stirred something deep in her mind, but the more she tried to pin it down, the more it eluded her. She sighed with frustration.

'Don't try to rush things. Just relax. You'll remember more that way—it worked for the riding, didn't it?'

She took his advice, and for the rest of the ride, concentrated on the beauty of the surroundings. They were passing through a cleared section of land dotted with river red gums which Talan pointed out to her. 'The first settlers believed those trees were a sign of good sheep grazing land.'

She nodded. 'They were right, too.'

Beyond a grove of eucalyptus trees, they disturbed a group of emus, peacefully grazing. They rode closer, but only when they were within yards of the birds, did they start to amble away.

Once, they came upon a group of stockmen working a mob of the splendid merino sheep which were Yarrakina's pride. Joselin watched, entranced as the bright-faced kelpies worked around the edges of the mob, dropping to their bellies then starting up and racing off after any sheep which dared to stray. Most of the men worked on motor bikes, on the back of which were wooden boxes which, Talan told her, the dogs rode in when they weren't working.

'But you prefer to work on horseback,' she hazarded.

'Maybe I'm the old-fashioned type,' he shrugged.

'No, I'd say you prefer the feeling of teamwork you get with a living creature, which you can't have with a petrol engine.'

He laughed. 'So now you're psycho-analysing me. But you could be right at that.'

The bleats of the sheep grew fainter as they rode on, then she tensed as they came within sight of a rocky outcrop rising out of the middle of the valley. 'Can we stop here?' she asked urgently.

He gave her an enquiring look. 'Any special reason? We can rest when we reach the Cave of Hands.'

'Please, I want to stop here.'

Reluctantly, he reined in his horse. She did the same and slid out of the saddle, dropping the horse's reins over its head. Then, as if mesmerised, she walked towards the foot of the outcrop.

'What's so special about this hunk of rock?' Talan asked, but there was an edge of tension in his voice.

She couldn't have said how she came by the knowledge, but she was quite certain. 'This is the rock I tried to jump off, isn't it?' she asked.

'What makes you think so?'

'Isn't it?' she repeated insistently.

'All right, so it is. Do you have some sort of morbid curiosity about it?'

'I don't really know why I wanted to stop here. Maybe to try and find some answers.' All the time, she was walking steadily towards the rock, her eyes scanning the base for something, *anything* which would tell her why she had tried to throw herself off this forbidding peak.

'Why didn't you tell me I tried to kill myself, or that you saved me?' she asked as she walked.

'I suppose I didn't really want to believe it,' he

admitted. 'I still can't accept that you would do such a cowardly thing.'

'Maybe I was driven to it,' she said lightly. She drew a sharp breath as he caught her by the elbow and wrenched her around to face him.

'Whatever it was, it wasn't by me,' he growled.

Frightened, she pulled away. 'I didn't say it was.'

His conscience must be troubling him, she thought as she continued her exploration of the outcrop. Why else would he be so defensive?

Something bumped against her foot and she kicked the undergrowth aside to find a flattened cardboard box buried in the brush. Bending down, she pushed more of the branches aside to reveal a layer of the boxes spread out along the base of the outcrop. 'Do you know what these are doing here?' she asked Talan as he came up behind her.

'I've no idea. Do you think you brought them here?'

'I don't know,' she said, feeling tears well dangerously close to the surface. The flattened boxes meant something, she was sure. If only she could remember what it was! But try as she might, no explanation came.

After a while, Talan put a hand on her shoulder. 'We'd better be going. This doesn't seem to be doing you any good.'

'But it should, I just know it.' Reluctantly, she got to her feet and followed Talan back to where the horses were grazing peacefully under a red gum.

The puzzle of the boxes continued to taunt her as they rode on. Once, Talan rode abreast of her and reached across to pat her hand. 'Don't try too hard, it will come,' he told her.

It was all right for him. He wasn't a stranger to his own past. It was like standing outside a locked door, knowing you had the key somewhere but being unable to find it. This time, however, she had the feeling she could push the door open if only she could find the strength. The truth was tantalisingly close. Maybe Talan's special place would hold the key.

They left the horses in a clearing, happily cropping the grass, then continued on foot down a white sand path and around a massive outcropping of huge rocks to a sheltered overhang of rocks which had once been a cave.

'So this is your special place,' she said in awe.

He watched her expectantly but when she showed no signs of recognition, his shoulders slumped. 'Don't you remember it at all?' he asked, disappointment in his tone.

She shot him a look of appeal. 'I wish I could, but . . .'

'I know. Nothing.'

In a mood of hopelessness, he walked with her around the shallow cave, pointing out the stencilled hands of long-vanished tribesmen, women and children who had left their marks here.

'The artist used red ochre, fat, water and a few other things mixed to a paste and held in his mouth, then he sprayed it over the rock to outline his hand,' he explained.

'But why choose only hands?' she asked in wonder.

'Nobody knows. There's another much more famous cave like this one in the Victoria Range, but it's been so badly vandalised that it has to be fenced off from visitors. This is the first intact one discovered this century.'

'Did you find it?'

'Your Aunt Pixie did, on one of her safaris into the ranges. She's found a number of aboriginal shelters to add to the forty or so known examples in the Grampians. It's a passion of hers.'

'And she wanted me to share it? I hardly know what to say.'

'Actually, she meant it as a gift to both of us,' he explained. 'She wanted us to be the first to see it before it's opened to the public.'

Deeply moved, she stared around at the hundreds of hands of all sizes—men's, women's and children's—which crowded the walls. Centuries of tribal tradition were recorded here, the message lost even to modern-day aboriginals. 'You said it was a gift to us,' she repeated. 'Does that mean there was something between you and me which Pixie wanted to help us celebrate?'

'Are you guessing or can you remember something?' he asked, his eyes alight with such hope that she wondered what he was waiting for her to remember.

She hated to disappoint him but she had no choice. 'No, I can't remember. It seemed as though there must be some special reason for Pixie to give us such a gift jointly.'

Disheartened, he turned away and rested his hand against the painted surface, accidentally placing it in the stencilled outline of another ancient palm. Absently, Joselin placed her own hand against a smaller, more feminine outline directly alongside Talan's. 'Do you think they were lovers in the Dreamtime?' she asked.

He took his hand away and crushed her to him in the confined space, pressing his mouth against hers hungrily, as if he never intended to let her go. At first, she was caught by surprise, then she gave herself up to the torrent of sensations surging through her body. He must mean something to her. He must. There was no other explanation for the overwhelming effect he had on her when he kissed her like this.

Willingly she kissed him back, parting her lips to

allow his probing tongue entry into the moist cavern of her mouth. When their tongues met, she gave a gasp of surprise and pleasure. Their bodies were moulded into one line and she knew they were dangerously close to making love right here, in the ancient cave. But she couldn't give in to him now any more than she could have last night. This wasn't the answer.

'Please, Talan, let me go,' she implored, her breath mingling with his, so close was his mouth to hers.

'You don't mean it. Let me love you and then you'll remember,' he implored.

In anguish, she pulled away. 'Remember what? You've got to stop talking in riddles and tell me what it is I'm supposed to remember about you. Tell me, were we having an affair?'

The light of desire which had been in his eyes, faded abruptly. 'I suppose Tony used that as an excuse to break it off with you.'

'You're impossible!' she seethed. 'I keep telling you that there was nothing between Tony and me. There never has been.'

'That's what he told you, anyway.'

'It's what I believe,' she corrected. 'Do you think I wouldn't recognise a lover if I saw one? There was nothing like that between Tony and me. If there was, I could feel it.'

'And what do you feel when you're with me?'

She spread her hands wide in a gesture of bewilderment. 'Confused. Frustrated. Knowing there's more to our relationship than you're telling me. Did we have an affair? Is that what Sonia's so hostile about?'

'We never made love,' he said flatly.

She looked at him blankly. 'Is that all?'

'Isn't it enough? You wanted to know if we'd had an

affair and the answer is no. I wanted you in my bed but you managed to stay out of it, even though we spent several nights together.'

'So you tried and failed, and now you blame me for it,' she said bleakly. 'There must have been a reason why I wouldn't let you make love to me.' God knows, I want to now, she added to herself, feeling the sexual tension like a living thing between them.

'You never did me the honour of explaining,' he said coldly and walked away from her.

She looked at his retreating back in despair. 'Why won't you tell me anything more?' she entreated.

He turned briefly. 'It's better for both of us if you remember on your own.'

'But what if I don't?'

He shrugged. 'Then maybe some things are best forgotten.'

Was he trying to tell her that he didn't want to go back to whatever their old relationship had been? It was the first time this thought had occurred to her and she wondered why she hadn't thought of it before. Maybe he regretted his fling with her, and wanted only to go back to Sonia whom he intended to marry. Perhaps he saw Joselin's amnesia as a heaven-sent way of wiping the slate clean between them.

If that was true, why had he bothered to bring her back here and take the risk of her memory returning? 'I hate you, Talan Devereaux,' she whispered to the ghosts in the cave.

'You're a liar, Joselin Pride,' they whispered back at her and to her shame, she knew they were right.

CHAPTER TEN

IT was mid-afternoon by the time they got back to the homestead, having ridden most of the way in chilly silence.

Talan curtly refused her offer to prepare some lunch for him, saying that he would help himself to something later. Then he disappeared into his study and soon afterwards, she heard the muted tapping of his computer keyboard. It was all very well for him. He could lose himself in the running of the property. How was she supposed to occupy her time?

Rather than show him how hurt she was by his refusal to tell her any more about their past relationship, she bustled around the kitchen, banging pots and pans together defiantly. In the end, however, instead of cooking anything, she made herself a triple decker salad sandwich.

As she ladled mayonnaise on to the top layer, she had a sudden vision of an unhappy little girl stuffing herself with cream cakes. Somehow, she knew the child was herself. She must make a habit of using food as a source of comfort, she concluded. She took the sandwich, a glass of mineral water and a paperback book out on to the terrace and settled down to read, but the print kept blurring in front of her eyes.

The memory of the cardboard boxes arranged at the foot of the outcrop where she had supposedly tried to kill herself, kept tugging at her. She was sure they must mean something. But the more she tried to remember, the more the explanation eluded her.

With a feeling of relief, she heard the telephone

shrill. Welcoming the diversion, she went back inside
to answer it and almost collided with Talan, intent on
the same errand. With mocking gesture, he deferred to
her and she picked it up, hoping it wasn't Tony to
further complicate things for her.

It was Sonia, calling from Stagwell. 'I'm having a
bit of car trouble, dear,' she said indulgently to
Joselin, using a tone better suited to addressing a small
child. 'Can you put Talan on for me?'

'Sure, he's right here,' she said ungraciously and
handed the receiver to him. 'It's Sonia.'

'Yes, love? What's the problem?'

Joselin didn't want to hear any more. Having him
call Sonia 'love' in that intimate tone was bad enough.
She didn't want to hear the rest of the conversation. It
would be just like Sonia to contrive some car trouble
to lure Talan to her resuce—and away from Joselin.

A few minutes later, he joined her in the living room
where she was pretending rapt interest in her book.
Her idle query about Sonia probably didn't fool him,
but why should she care? He had made his feelings
perfectly clear at the cave this afternoon.

'It's nothing serious,' he said in response to her
query. 'Her car started overheating between here and
Stawell. Sounds like a broken fan belt. I'll drive out
and take her a spare so she should be able to make it
back all right.'

'Regular knight in shining armour,' she sneered
sotto voce, but he had already gone upstairs. Soon
afterwards, wearing a leather jacket over his jeans, he
came down again and she heard him drive away.

Unhappily, she closed her book. She should have
known Sonia wouldn't leave them alone so readily.
Not that she had anything to worry about where
Joselin was concerned. From the little Talan had told
her at the cave this afternoon, there was nothing more

between them than sexual attraction—and even that had come to nothing, so he could go back to Sonia with a clear conscience.

Restlessly, she glanced at the clock. It was too early to retire to her room and her suitcase was already packed for the trip back to Melbourne. Talan had talked her out of going today, but she was determined not to put it off any longer. So how should she pass the time until Talan and Sonia returned?

Suddenly, she thought of the gourmet meals Sonia had been cooking for Talan since she arrived. Why not show him that Joselin was at least as creative a cook? It wasn't much, but it might make him remember her more kindly when she was gone.

Jumping up, she went back to the kitchen then stood looking around with indecision. The pantry and the big freezer were well stocked with ingredients, but she hadn't the slightest idea what to make. She recalled seeing a drawer crammed full of newspaper and magazine cuttings. Talan had explained that they were recipes which Aunt Pixie had always intended to paste into a scrapbook, but never had done. She might find inspiration there.

The recipes were in a hopeless jumble but she smoothed out several of the cuttings and glanced at them. Two of them, for Cream of Watercress Soup and Citrus Mousse, she kept aside. All she needed now was a main course. Then it came to her—why not use some of Yarrakina's own bounty and cook a rack of lamb?

The menu settled, she tried to close the drawer again, but it jammed half-open. One of the cuttings must be stuck at the back. She pulled the drawer all the way out and peered inside. There was a whole folded newspaper wedged between the drawer runners at the back. Tugging it free, she closed the drawer

again and glanced idly at the paper. It was the local
newspaper and dated a couple of weeks beforehand.

Suddenly her eye was riveted by her own name and
the room swam around her as she read the
surrounding text.

In a ceremony held at Stawell Hospital yesterday,
Miss Joselin Pride married Mr Talan Devereaux of
Yarrakina, at the bedside of Miss Pride's critically
ill aunt, local personality, Mrs Pixie Pride.

Officiating at the ceremony was marriage celebrant, Mr Anthony Briar, a friend of the bride, who
flew from Melbourne to conduct the wedding.

It didn't make sense! Surely if she was married to
Talan, he would have said something? But he had, she
recalled dizzily. 'We could be married,' he'd said so
casually that she assumed he was making a cruel joke.

All at once, the kitchen began to whirl around her
and she clutched a cabinet for support. There was a
roaring sound in her head, like surf pounding against
rocks. She felt as if she was going to faint. From
somewhere deep in her mind, she recalled the correct
first-aid for faintness—and stumbled to a chair,
forcing her head down between her knees.

Gradually, the roaring sound subsided and she
opened her eyes, lifting her head cautiously. But the
dizzy spell had passed. She no longer felt as if she was
going to collapse.

Her glass of mineral water was within reach and she
took a few steadying sips. She hadn't felt as bad as this
since she auditioned for a stunt job in which she was
to appear with John Wayne in a rare TV commercial
he made in Australia.

She hadn't felt this bad since . . . her eyes widened
as she realised what she was thinking. She was
remembering! 'I'm Joselin Pride, 26 years old and a

professional stunt woman,' she recited aloud in wonder.

With her returning memory came a full awareness of what her relationship with Talan was. Now she understood only too well why he had been unwilling to discuss it with her. He was so disgusted with her over the fake wedding that he didn't even want to remember it, far less encourage her to recall the details.

She almost laughed aloud. Talan didn't know that she was a stunt woman. No wonder he had thought she had been trying to kill herself when he had seen her preparing to jump from the outcrop. He couldn't have known that she did stunts like that all the time. Or at least, she had until a dreadful accident destroyed her nerve, she acknowledged, remembering it all now.

The chain of events was startlingly clear now. She had been preparing for a comeback after Tony offered her a part in a forthcoming film. Misunderstanding what she was doing, Talan had tried to stop her from jumping and had ruined her aim so she landed clumsily, taking him with her.

She shuddered as she remembered hitting her head on a rock, then—nothing. When she awoke in her bedroom at Yarrakina, she had been unable to remember anything until this moment. A lot of good it would do her now, she thought bitterly. Talan's words at the cave were only too clear in her mind. 'Some things are best forgotten.' Was that what he preferred to do? Now that their liason had served its purpose in helping Pixie to get well, there was no need for it to continue. He could return to Sonia as if Joselin had never existed. If Sonia had her way, that's what would happen. And Joselin got the feeling that Sonia usually had her way.

She looked around the kitchen. Now that her

memory had returned, she was tempted to get into her car and head straight back to Melbourne. But she still felt shaky from the shock so it probably wouldn't be wise to try to drive at all, far less such a distance.

She decided to continue preparing dinner for Talan and Sonia. It would be her last chance to show off for him at Yarrakina, so she may as well make the most of it. If she ever came again, Sonia would be mistress here.

The prospect filled her with despair. If only she hadn't been such a fool, asking Tony to play the part of a marriage celebrant, she could have been Talan's wife now, looking forward to a future here at his side.

Yet what sort of future would it have been? It was obvious that he would never have asked Joselin to marry him if he hadn't been desperate to help Pixie. He didn't care for her any more now than he had when they were children on holiday here. If she had married him, he would have come to hate having her forced upon him—especially if it was Sonia he wanted all along.

'This has got to stop,' she said to the empty kitchen. She couldn't go on feeling sorry for herself, so she may as well accept things as they were. At least she had her work to go back to, now that she was well and strong again. Once she was back in harness she could forget all about Talan. It might take some time—a long, long time, she acknowledged—but anything was possible if you set your mind to it.

In a frenzy of activity, she took three rib loin roasts of lamb out of the freezer and set them to defrost in the microwave. Then she prepared a marinade of lemon juice and seasoning with which to baste the roasts when they were ready. By then the racks of lamb had thawed sufficiently for her to baste them with the marrinade and pop them into a hot oven. By the time they were golden brown, Talan should be back, with Sonia following in her own car.

Then she set about chopping vegetables for the soup. That done, she dissolved lemon and orange juice in gelatine and beat a mixture of egg whites and cream through it to make a tangy, foaming dessert. As an afterthought, she set mandarin slices to marinate in Cointreau to decorate the dessert. Let Sonia top that! she thought defiantly.

She should have remembered the best-laid plans of mice and men, because three hours later, there was still no sign of Talan or Sonia. The roast was a shrivelled dark brown lump in the oven. Miserably, she turned it off and removed the pot of soup from the stove. An unappetising skin had formed on top. Hadn't she expected something like this? Determined to keep them apart, Sonia must have persuaded Talan to take her to dinner in Stawell.

When sunset came, she heard the stockmen returning to their quarters, their laughter heightening her sense of loneliness. But no one came to the main house and finally, she went up to bed.

Hours later, she was disturbed by sounds on the landing outside her room. 'Is that yo, Talan?' she called timidly, her heart thudding.

'It's me, sorry to waken you,' came Sonia's whispered response.

Joselin's heart sank. So Sonia and Talan had spent the entire evening together in town, only returning in the early hours of the morning. Would she ever get used to thinking of them as a pair?

She awoke next morning in the same sad frame of mind, unable to pinpoint its cause until she remembered her solitary evening. Well, enough was enough. She wasn't spending one more night playing gooseberry to those two.

Throwing back the bedclothes, she leapt out of bed, relieved to find it was only just dawn and the air held the promise of a fine, clear morning. She showered and dressed speedily, glad that her things were already packed. With luck, she could be away from here before Talan and Sonia awoke. Leaving them a note would save a lot of explanations.

But luck wasn't with her. She emerged on to the landing, suitcase in hand, just as Sonia came out of Talan's room. The other woman was dressed in a plum-coloured velour robe and her eyes were still hooded with sleep. 'So you're leaving?' she said, eyeing Joselin's case. Pointedly, she pulled Talan's bedroom door shut behind her—to avoid waking him, Joselin guessed. The thought of them sharing a bed wounded her almost beyond bearing, but there was little she could do about it.

'Yes, I'm going back to Melbourne,' she confirmed, then some imp of mischief made her add, 'I remembered everything last night. Your ring is on the table in the living room.'

If she expected Sonia to be ashamed, she was disappointed. The other woman merely shrugged philosophically. 'It's a shame you weren't really engaged to Tony Briar, then everything would have been much simpler.'

Simpler for whom? Joselin wondered but said nothing. All she wanted now was to get out of here as quickly as possible. 'Will you . . .' she choked on the words, '. . . will you tell Talan I said goodbye.'

'I'll tell him,' Sonia said evenly.

She remained standing at the top of the stairs as Joselin made her way down. She was tempted to look back as she reached the front door, then thought better of it and went quickly outside to her car.

The dawn was unfolding from pink to yellow and

gold as she walked towards the carports. Quicksilver
whinnied to her and she felt a lump rise in her throat.
'No more wild rides for us, fellow,' she said, patting
the horse's silky nose as she passed.

As she drove down the winding gravel driveway
towards the main road, the dawn flooded the purple hills
and the bleached blond pastures with soft light. As it
kissed the tops of the eucalypts, birds burst into song.

She was going to miss Yarrakina, she admitted to
herelf. She had come here to find herself but had
found much more than she had bargained for. Falling
in love hadn't been part of her plans, but that's what
she had done and it would be a long time before she
experienced its like again, if she ever did, she thought
ruefully. In the film world, there weren't many men
like Talan Devereaux.

Come to think of it, there weren't many men like
him in any world. Fool that she was, she had thrown
away the chance to have him for herself, and now it
was too late.

Now, he belonged to Sonia. Thinking of the other
woman, sloe-eyed and fresh from Talan's bed, was
acutely painful, so Joselin made an effort to
concentrate on the driving. She didn't want a
repetition of the accident which had brought her and
Talan together in the first place, so she kept a watchful
eye out for kangaroos. She saw one or two bounding
along the skyline, but none came close to the road.

Soon, she was approaching Stawell. It was much too
early to go straight to the hospital so she located a cafe
which opened early to cater for truck drivers passing
through the town. Here, she ordered scrambled eggs,
toast and coffee and forced herself to eat the meal, to
fortify herself for the long drive back to Melbourne.

By the time she had eaten, the town was beginning
to stir and she decided to try her luck at the hospital.

Fortunately, Dr Hastings was already there and greeted her in the corridor. 'You're bright and early.'

'I . . . I have to go back to Melbourne right away and I was wondering if I could visit Pixie,' she said. 'I know it isn't visiting hours yet, but . . .'

He winked conspiratorially. 'Since she's in a private room, you won't be disturbing other patients so I don't see why not.' He looked over his shoulder, miming fear. 'Just don't let Sister know I let you in.'

She laughed in spite of herself. 'Your secret is safe with me.'

Pixie was sitting up in bed reading a morning paper when she went in. Her eyes lit up when she saw Joselin. 'My, this is a pleasant surprise. When did you get back from Melbourne?'

Joselin had forgotten that she was supposed to have been away for the last few days. 'I . . . er . . . I'm only here on a flying visit,' she improvised. 'I have to go straight back.'

'Does that mean you got the part?' Pixie asked.

'Er . . . no, I didn't. You see . . .'

'Actually, I'm pleased to hear it,' Pixie said, surprising Joselin. 'I'm sorry you're disappointed of course, but I hope now you will decide to settle down at Yarrakina with Talan. I know you girls see things differently nowadays, but I still believe a woman's place is with her husband.'

Lacking the heart to deceive Pixie any longer, Joselin sat down on the edge of the bed and took her aunt's hand. 'There's something I have to tell you about Talan and me.'

Pixie looked expectant. 'Yes, dear, what is it?'

There was a disturbance at the door, then a voice interrupted. 'What Joselin is trying to say is that we want you to come and live with us at Yarrakina when you leave hospital next week.'

Startled, Joselin looked up to see Talan standing in the doorway. She was shocked by the change in him since yesterday. His eyes were red-rimmed, a dark shadow stubbled his chin and his clothes were crumpled, as if he had slept in them last night.

'Talan!' she gasped, then remembering Pixie's presence, she gasped, 'I didn't expect to see you here this early.'

'So I gathered, he said drily, and slumped into a chair across the room. 'I meant what I said, Pixie,' he repeated.

The elderly woman's eyes glowed and there was the sparkle of tears in them, which she wiped away impatiently. 'Are you sure you want me to live with you?' When he nodded, she said, 'You don't know how much this means to me.'

Talan stood up. 'It means much more to us to have you with us. Yarrakina just wouldn't be the same without you. Who would take care of the aboriginal shelters and look for new ones? We need you there.'

No other words could have affected Aunt Pixie more. She wept unashamedly then, clutching his hand while Joselin looked helplessly from her aunt to Talan. How could he say such a thing, when he knew the true situation between them? It wasn't fair to raise Pixie's hopes like this when he knew they would have to be dashed.

Unless . . . a new thought occurred to her. Perhaps he had been able to persuade Sonia to allow Pixie to live at Yarrakina? Joselin knew she would leave with a much lighter heart if she could believe that. It would mean so much to her to know that her aunt was happy and well cared for.

'Just what do you think you're doing?' came an irate voice. The ward sister bustled in and looked at them disapprovingly.

'Dr Hastings gave us permission to call in,' Joselin explained, mentally apologising to the doctor for giving him away.

'Well, you'll have to run along now,' the sister said, but there was a twinkle of understanding in her eyes, belying the stern demeanour. 'The business of the hospital can't grind to a halt every time someone feels like dropping in.'

'Of course not. We're very sorry, sister,' Talan said so meekly that Joselin was tempted to laugh. He took her arm and urged her towards the door. 'We'll see you later, Pixie—during proper visiting hours.'

He held firmly to her arm all the way through the building and outside in the car-park. When she tried to pull free his grip tightened. 'Where do you think you're going.'

'My car's parked over here.'

'It will be quite safe there while we take a little ride in mine,' he said evenly.

'Now just a minute, I'm not going anywhere with you! Haven't you done enough damage by telling Pixie she can come and live with us—when you know perfectly well that there isn't any "us"?'

He crooked an eyebrow. 'Isn't there? When I phoned home a few minutes ago, Sonia gave me to understand that you'd regained your memory, so you should recall that we're married.'

Was he trying to force her to confirm what he already knew? 'All right,' she said heavily, 'I admit I tricked you into thinking we were married. Is that what you're waiting to hear? If it is, all I can say is I'm more sorry than you'll ever know.'

'Sorry that you agreed to marry me?' he queried tensely.

'No!' It was out before she could stop herself. 'Only sorry that I deceived you.'

'As long as that's your only regret, there's some hope for us,' he observed. He was still steering her through the car-park, and stopped when he reached his Mercedes, opening the door to let her slide into the passenger seat.

'Where are we going?' she asked when he got into the driver's side. While he was walking around to the other side of the car, she toyed briefly with running back to her own car, but curiosity got the better of her. He wasn't acting like someone who despised her at all. More like . . . her brain refused to consider the alternative.

'I'm taking you somewhere quiet, where we can talk,' he said, concentrating on the driving.

'I don't know what we have to talk about.'

In the driving mirror, she saw him frown. 'Our future will do for starters, don't you think?'

She didn't know they had one, so she subsided into thoughtful silence for the rest of the journey. Leaving the hospital, they drove along Patrick Street, which was notable for being the first thoroughfare in the town to have street lighting. Passing the handsome old freestone courthouse, they made several turns until they passed the trotting track, reclaimed from a mine tailings dump. They were driving up to Pioneers' Lookout, she realised.

Sure enough, soon afterwards, Talan brought the car to a halt on top of Big Hill, recognised from earliest times as one of the best vantage points from which to overlook the town and surrounding countryside. The area was rich in gold-mining history, being the first place where gold-bearing quartz was discovered during the goldrush. But history was the farthest thing from her mind as Talan switched off the engine and swivelled towards her, sliding his hand along the back of the seat so she was achingly conscious of it inches from her cheek.

'Why have you brought me here?' she asked nervously. 'If it's an apology you want, I've already told you I'm sorry.'

'I know—sorry you deceived me, but not sorry that you agreed to marry me.'

'You don't seem very angry either way.'

'I admit, I was very shaken when Sonia showed me the newspaper article and told me what you'd done. Frankly, it seemed like my mother's scheming behaviour all over again. Then I asked myself why you would do such a thing. I felt sure there was more to the story than the way Sonia made it appear. If I'd thought to ask Pixie for your Melbourne address at that stage, I would have gone there much sooner and sorted the whole thing out.'

She was bewildered. 'You had enough faith in me to want to go to Melbourne to find out the truth?' It seemed almost too good to be true.

'Better than that, I finally got there, but not until it was almost too late.' His hand slid down the leather seat and caressed her cheek with such gentleness that it sent a shudder of longing through her. 'Why didn't you tell me that you were a professional stunt woman, instead of letting me think you were a fluffy-headed actress?'

Haltingly, she explained about the accident, stumbling a little over the details but willing herself not to leave anything out. Having learned this much of her story, he deserved to know it all before they parted. 'So my doctor advised me to get away for a while, where nobody knew what I did for a living. He said that as long as people knew I was a stunt woman, they would expect more of me than I was able to deliver at the time.'

She laughed self-deprecatingly. 'He told me I have an unconscious need to be protected but I was fighting it by trying to be the original Miss Independence. I wasn't the least bit independent when I came here. Any little thing could reduce me to a jelly.'

'But not any more.' It was a statement rather than a question.

'No, not now. Staying at Yarrakina gave me my courage back.'

He seemed disappointed. 'So it was only being back at Yarrakina that did the trick?'

Out of stubborn pride, she was tempted to let him think so but she couldn't deceive him any further. 'No, it wasn't the property—it was you,' she said simply. 'You had such faith in me that it restored my faith in myself. The more I worried about you, the less I worried about what I could or couldn't do and before I knew it, I was in full command of myself again.'

'So your so-called suicide attempt was really a comeback, wasn't it?'

She nodded. 'I knew those cardboard boxes at the base of the outcrop were a clue. It was the landing stage I'd set up for myself.'

He drew a sharp breath. 'If I hadn't come along and tried to play hero and save you, you wouldn't have been hurt.'

With a gentle finger, she traced the fading bruise on his cheek. 'You paid for your heroics, too, remember?'

He shook his head. 'But not as high a price as you did, or as high as the one we both nearly paid.'

'What price?' she asked, her throat tight with anticipation.

'The loss of each other.'

She could hardly believe what she was hearing. 'You mean there's still a chance for us after all?' she whispered.

His arm which rested along the seat behind her,

dropped on to her shoulder and he pulled her close. 'There is if you want it.'

She looked up at him with adoring eyes. 'I want it more than anything else in the world. But I was sure I'd ruined everything when I pretended to marry you.'

'I admit I was furious when I first found out. When I thought you loved Tony Briar, I was sure you'd invited him to perform the ceremony as a way of bringing him to heel, then when it didn't work, you'd tried to kill yourself.'

She could see how this explanation appeared to fit the facts as he knew them. 'I hope now you'll accept that there's nothing between Tony and me, and never was?' she insisted.

'I believe it now. When I met Julie Simpson at your flat in Melbourne, it was obvious that she and Tony have eyes for no one but each other.'

'What I don't understand, is what you hoped to achieve in Melbourne?'

He looked abashed. 'I had the crazy idea that I could persuade Tony to come back to you. The way you defended him when I threw him out that day at Yarrakina, I thought you still loved him. If I couldn't have you, then I wanted you to have a chance at happiness.'

Her heart sang as she realised he couldn't possibly have spent the night with Sonia. He must have driven all night to get to Melbourne and back by this morning. 'Oh, Talan, I could never be happy with anyone but you,' she told him.

'Do you mean that, my darling?'

'With all my heart.'

'Then you will marry me—for real this time?'

She wrinkled her brow in puzzlement. 'But what about Sonia?'

He let out a whistling breath of impatience. 'I

already told you that Sonia doesn't come into it. She's looking for a property to marry, not a man. When I found out that she'd staged her car breakdown yesterday to make me dance attendance on her, I told her it wasn't going to work. I sent her back to Yarrakina to pack. She'll be shopping for a new landowner by tomorrow.'

Something still didn't make sense. 'But what about the night you spent with her in Stawell? Pixie told me you'd both been to visit her next day.'

'So we had, but not together. That day, I left Yarrakina in a fury after finding that Wizzard character waiting for you, seemingly knowing things about your personal life that only a lover could know. I didn't even know that Sonia had followed me to Stawell until hours later. We certainly weren't together.'

'Garth Vizzard is a private investigator for an insurance company,' she explained. She told Talan about the man's relentless efforts to prove she was faking the effects of her accident in order to gain a large sum of money from his company.

Talan nodded in understanding. 'I began to suspect there was something odd about him when I saw him in Stawell the same night, having dinner with Sonia. Jealous as I was, even I could see that no lover would desert a girl like you for someone else in such haste.'

Ignoring the rest, she seized on one phrase. 'You were jealous of Garth Vizzard?'

'I'm jealous of any man who comes between you and me,' he said gruffly, tightening his hold on her. 'I always have been.'

'Yet you never gave me a clue!'

'How could I? When I first realised my feelings for you, you were little more than a child. Besides, you were always so self-contained, you never gave me any encouragement.'

'I guess I was protecting myself even then,' she mused. 'I'd been so hurt by the break-up of my parents' marriage that I was determined not to leave myself open to any more pain. So I told myself you didn't want a kid like me around, and set out to make it true by being as unapproachable as possible.'

'And stuffing yourself with cakes to make yourself fat and ugly,' he teased.

'Can't you ever forget that?' she wailed. 'I outgrew that sort of behaviour years ago.' If you don't count triple decker salad sandwiches, she thought guiltily. 'Surely you must have some weaknesses, yourself?'

'Oh, I do,' he agreed solemnly. 'The greatest of them is right here beside me.'

So saying, he pulled her across his knees and brought his mouth hard down against hers. Alarm flickered in her breast as she felt the stirring of his need for her, then she told herself that nothing could be as right as the way she felt now in his arms.

After a long time, he drew his mouth away from hers reluctantly, but kept her cradled in his arms. 'I want to marry you, Joselin—for real this time. I don't care if you go on jumping off cliffs for a living, as long as you come back to Yarrakina in between times.'

She smiled langorously. 'I don't know how much jumping off cliffs one can do while pregnant. And Yarrakina is just asking for hordes of children.'

'Does that mean you'll marry me?'

'Yes, oh yes,' she breathed. 'But . . . what shall we tell Pixie? She thinks we *are* married.'

'I know. We'll say nothing until she's well enough then tell her the truth. Knowing Pixie, she'll understand why we did it. I'm sure Dr Hastings will, too.'

Suddenly, Talan frowned. 'There's one condition I insist on, however.'

Mildly alarmed, she tried to sit up but was held firmly in his arms. 'What is it?'

He looked at her long and hard, then smiled. 'I get to choose the preacher this time.'

'Oh you!'

Then she was silenced by a deep, demanding kiss which sent waves of excitement surging through her, reminding her that no ceremony could bind them more closely than the love they already shared.

Here's how to get this special offer from Harlequin!

November
**BETTY NEELS
TREASURY EDITION
COUPON**

As simple as 1…2…3!

1. **Each month, save one Treasury Edition coupon from your favorite Romance or Presents novel.**
2. **In four months you'll have saved four Treasury Edition coupons (only one coupon per month allowed).**
3. **Then all you have to do is fill out and return the order form provided, along with the four Treasury Edition coupons required and $2.95 for postage and handling.**

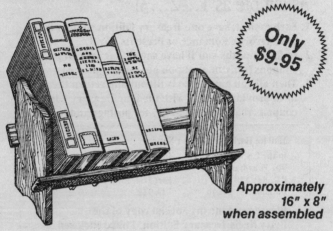